Hope was going to have a baby.

Lyon's heart thud football field.

"Who says anyon___ condition? For the ___ Hope added to his arched look.

"Are you suggesting we pass the baby off as mine?" he asked slowly.

"Maybe I'm splitting hairs, but I was thinking that if we're not announcing a pregnancy, there's no deception."

After staring at her for several seconds, he abruptly glanced at his watch and muttered an expletive under his breath. "I have to get back to the station. Forgive me," he began. "I'm admittedly tired, a little cranky and feeling way out of my comfort zone. Humor me and let me do at least one thing conventionally." Awkwardly shifting the bag into his bandaged left hand, he placed three fingers under her chin and tilted her face upward. "Marry me?" he asked.

"Yes," she whispered.

Dear Reader,

Happy spring! Hope and Lyon's story begins in May, as well. Actually, it began when they were both schoolkids, but as life and fate would have it, they never got to follow through on impulses and deep-seated feelings until heartache and heartbreak changed everything.

As I was developing their story, I was reminded of my first book for Silhouette Books, *Partners for Life* for the Desire series, which became a Golden Medallion (now RITA® Award) nominee. It, too, echoed a theme from O. Henry's famous short story, *The Gift of the Magi,* where a couple make sacrifices for love.

This is my 44th book and it seems fitting after all that has occurred these past few years that there's a sense of having come full circle. My sincere thanks to those of you who have stayed with me through the journey, especially those who have written to ask for specific stories. I hope I can fulfill those requests.

Know that you are imperative in what we do. So from the bottom of my heart, thank you for being readers! I wish you all a personal love story to equal Hope and Lyon's.

With warmest regards,

Helen

HOPE'S CHILD

HELEN R. MYERS

Silhouette

SPECIAL EDITION®

Published by Silhouette Books

America's Publisher of Contemporary Romance

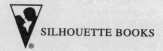

SILHOUETTE BOOKS

Recycling programs
for this product may
not exist in your area.

ISBN-13: 978-0-373-65527-4

HOPE'S CHILD

Visit Silhouette Books at www.eHarlequin.com

Printed in U.S.A.

Books by Helen R. Myers

Silhouette Special Edition

After That Night... #1066
Beloved Mercenary #1162
What Should Have Been #1758
A Man to Count On #1830
The Last Man She'd Marry #1914
Daddy on Demand #2004
Hope's Child #2045

Silhouette Romance

Donovan's Mermaid #557
Someone To Watch Over Me #643
Confidentially Yours #677
Invitation to a Wedding #737
A Fine Arrangement #776
Through My Eyes #814
Three Little Chaperones #861
Forbidden Passion #908
A Father's Promise #1002
To Wed at Christmas #1049
The Merry Matchmaker #1121
Baby in a Basket #1169

Silhouette Books

Silhouette Shadows Collection 1992
"Seawitch"

Montana Mavericks
The Law is No Lady

Silhouette Desire

Partners for Life #370
Smooth Operator #454
That Fontaine Woman! #471
The Pirate O'Keefe #506
Kiss Me Kate #570
After You #599
When Gabriel Called #650
Navarrone #738
Jake #797
Once Upon a Full Moon #857
The Rebel and the Hero #941
Just a Memory Away #990
*The Officer and the
    Renegade* #1102

Silhouette Shadows

Night Mist #6
Whispers in the Woods #23
Watching for Willa #49

MIRA Books

Come Sundown
More Than You Know
Lost
Dead End
Final Stand
No Sanctuary
While Others Sleep

HELEN R. MYERS

is a collector of two- and four-legged strays, and lives deep in the Piney Woods of East Texas. She cites cello music and bonsai gardening as favorite relaxation pastimes, and still edits in her sleep—an accident, learned while writing her first book. A bestselling author of diverse themes and focus, she is a three-time RITA® Award nominee, winning for *Navarrone* in 1993.

Prologue

"Would you hand over your truck keys, please?"

Right after sliding into the back booth of the Cedar Grove Bar and Grill, Hope Alessandro Harrell got the exact reaction she expected from her fiancé, Will Nichols. His baby blues widened, he reared back his blond head as though startled by an unexpected jab, and then he smirked.

"Now darlin', you aren't going to make a scene, are you?"

Blinking away tears of humiliation from what she'd witnessed upon entering the North Central Texas establishment, she enunciated softly to avoid being overheard by the diners around them, "You've put on enough of a show for one night, and I don't care to sit here a second longer than I have to being either pitied or gossiped about. Now, either pass me the keys to your truck, or I'll call someone to get a lift home...or ask Lyon to drive me." She regretted accepting a friend's offer to drop her off so she could drive back to her place with Will. What had seemed a good idea at the time—due to the weather—was suddenly a major error in judgment.

By "Lyon," she meant Chief of Police Lyon Teague still standing by the bar pretending to nurse a mug of coffee. Will's old schoolmate and best friend had stopped by to escape the May downpour that was making driving in their area treacherous. He had obviously witnessed what had transpired before her arrival, since he'd been standing beside Will when she'd entered. From the expression on his face, he, too, was wishing he was anywhere but there.

"And how am *I* supposed to get home?" Will asked. "I have two hundred head of cattle to transfer to the sale barns first thing tomorrow morning."

"Ask Rochelle Sims to give you a lift. I've no doubt as soon as I leave, she'll be all over you again anyway."

Will's bored expression spoke fathoms about how seriously he was taking this. "Rochelle is just…Rochelle."

Although there wasn't a hint of a slur to his speech to confirm that he'd been drinking for a while before she'd arrived, his attitude made Hope all the more offended and disgusted. "And that's acceptable behavior to you? Her hands all over you—in places no *lady* should venture in public?"

"Now you're exaggerating."

"I don't think so. I also don't think this was the first time she's been so familiar with you."

Aware that there were a good dozen people angling to see and listen to what was going on between them, Hope leaned across the table and extended her hand. "I'm dead serious, Will. Keys. Either way, I'm out of here."

Muttering, Will handed them over, but when she slid out

of the booth, she wasn't thrilled that he followed. At six-four he could pretty well go wherever he wanted to go, and being only five-seven in her highest heels, Hope felt compelled to pause by Lyon before exiting the grill.

"I'd just like you to know that we're leaving. I'll be driving myself home in Will's truck to my place. A friend dropped me off so I'm without a ride. Could you make sure he gets home okay once he takes possession of his vehicle?"

Shooting Will a grim look, Lyon opened his mouth to speak, then, paused and nodded once. "I'll do better than that, I'll be right behind you."

Hope sensed from Lyon's demeanor that what he really wanted was for her to let him drive her home. But she still had things to say to Will; they might as well get it over with than drag things out. Relieved to know that Lyon would be close, she touched the sleeve of his yellow police raincoat. "I appreciate that."

It was early May and spring was exhibiting its more serious side with a rock-and-roll thunderstorm. Lightning shot from black skies like laser guns in a sci-fi movie and the earth shook as bolts hit in frequent succession. The storm had stalled, so as soon as a bolt exploded in the east, another struck the pasture across the street, and before Hope could swallow her heart back down into her chest, the western sky lit followed by a hair-raising crack. Any thought of backing out of her decision to delay her departure was gone as the restaurant's door shut behind them indicating Will was blocking her retreat. Hope ran for the truck. Unfortunately, along with her high heels, she was in a pencil skirt, so when Will caught up with her and snatched the keys out of her hands, she could do nothing but shout his name in protest.

"Get inside before we both get fried!" he yelled back to her.

By the time she slammed the passenger door shut, she was as angry as she was drenched. Once Will climbed in on the driver's side, she snapped, "I swear, Will, this is it."

In truth, though, she was as fed up with herself than she was with him; after all, he was just being himself. She was the fool for believing that loving her would inspire some maturity and restraint in the man. At this point she had to wonder if he knew what the meaning of love truly meant? Even as he backed out of the parking slot and exited the lot, she could tell he was no less upset. But that was his perfect M.O. for being caught red-handed.

"The wedding is off," she continued, striving to keep her tone even.

Will's response was as if she'd thrown her engagement ring out the window. Swearing, he pounded the steering wheel with his fist. "That's not fair!"

"Oh, and playing touchy-feely with a woman who would lie with roadkill for a thrill is? What's unfair is that you've been misrepresenting yourself all along. How often did you cheat after dropping me off at home, or when I was out of town on business? Just count during this past year that we've been engaged."

"You can't expect me to answer such a lose-lose question. C'mon, baby, you know what happened back there was nothing."

"It was plenty something to me. Did you really think I was that desperate to get married that I would pretend to not notice your loose zipper mentality? Then you don't know me at all."

"Well, get it all out then and tell me what I need to do to

make you happy again because your father won't let you cancel the wedding," Will said, his tone resigned. "He wants Nichols land joined with Harrell land one way or another. Besides, I can't afford to pay him back what I owe him yet."

This second shock of the evening left Hope almost speechless. "You borrowed from my father knowing how he does business? When? How much?" The next troubling and infuriating thing to cross her mind was that her father hadn't said a word of this to her.

"Under the circumstances, it's none of your business, is it?"

He sounded more like a teenager focused on gaining the upper hand than an adult of thirty-four. "Right you are," Hope said telling herself that in the long run, she was about to get off easy. "Forget that I asked."

That indifference wasn't the reaction Will had expected. "Okay, so I goofed up and a couple of things didn't work out. The bank note was due last month, but cattle prices were too low to send them to market. Everything is fine now. I'll pay him back by Monday. You know, the bank was really impressed that I have you and your old man's support. They finally increased my line of credit, so I won't have to borrow from him again."

Hope experienced a new wave of revulsion for him. Why hadn't he let her see these anything-goes, means-to-an-end sides of him? Studying his profile for a few seconds, she announced. "I'm pregnant."

Will threw back his head and howled with glee. "Jackpot!"

That told Hope all she needed to know. She'd been taken off birth control by her doctor and Will had assured her that he would be responsible for taking care of things until she had made up her mind on the best means of protection, or was ready to start a family. They'd not had unprotected sex, so finding herself weeks late had rattled her, especially since historically her menstrual cycle was as regular as a government clock. "You tampered with those condoms," she said voicing her worst suspicion.

With a shrug and self-satisfied grin, Will replied, "It all works out. We wanted kids. I needed insurance in case something like this sprang up before the wedding."

Amazing, she thought. He was disciplined enough for all of these machinations, but he couldn't restrict himself to one woman—let alone be truthful to her.

"I can't wait to tell Ellis," Will continued.

"You do that." Seething, Hope's hand shook as she pulled off the engagement ring that had been feeling increasingly cumbersome and awkward on her hand. If he was having financial troubles, she could only imagine what he still owed on it. "And be sure to let him know that I'm done with you and why."

When she pulled open the ashtray drawer and dropped the ring inside, Will protested. "Hey! Put that back on!"

Hope couldn't believe when he began swatting away her hand and grappling for the piece of jewelry. "Watch the road, Will. *Will!*"

The big white dually pickup spun on the oil-and-water slick county road. Uttering an explicit curse, Will jerked on the steering wheel. That overreaction shot the diesel truck down an embankment where the truck's right wheels sunk quickly into ground already soft from two previous flooding rains. The momentum sent the weighty vehicle flipping into the pasture below.

As they rolled over and over, Hope screamed, first out of terror, next from the pain as Will's much larger and heavier body slammed repeatedly against hers. He'd been too agitated and too determined to get his way to fasten his seat belt.

When the 360-degree roller coaster came to a halt, they had settled upside down. Gasping to get air into her lungs as the seat belt threatened to slice her neck and crush her lungs from her body being forced against it, Hope's first thought was, *My baby!*

She knew she wouldn't be able to tell how badly she was hurt until she was upright again and prayed it was soon. Her body's blood was rushing to her head and she felt every heartbeat, the fresh night air rushing through all four shattered door windows reviving her more than she might have wanted. Then her gaze settled on the crumpled, still heap beside her.

"Will?"

He didn't respond, didn't move at all as he lay on the ceiling of the cab. In this rural field away from street lights, she couldn't tell if he was bleeding or even breathing. She reached for him.

"Will!"

"Hope—don't try to move him!"

The sound of Lyon's voice sent a wave of relief over her that brought tears to her eyes. She twisted what little she could to see him drop to his knees and lean down to peer at her. He aimed his flashlight all around her to gauge her condition, but tried to avoid getting the beam directly in her eyes. Grasping the hand she reached toward him, he squeezed reassuringly.

"Are you bleeding anywhere, sweetheart?"

"N-no. I don't think so. But Will—"

Lyon aimed the flashlight at him and after only three seconds, returned the beam to her. "Let's get you out first. I'm smelling fuel."

Come to think of it, Hope did, too. As a new wave of terror threatened to override reason, she repressed a whimper and wrestled with the seat belt.

"I've got it. Easy…"

Lyon opened a pocketknife and quickly sliced the belt. With his help, she slumped more than dropped to the padded ceiling. Then wrapping his arms around her, he eased her through the frame of sharp shards as quickly but carefully as he could.

"That's it," he said praising her instincts to fold into a fetal position to protect her face and extremities. In less than a minute from first arriving, he was jogging up the slope to his patrol car lighting the night sky with its own light show.

"Put me down, Lyon," she pleaded. "I'm okay and you need to get back to Will." But another close bolt of lightning made a liar out of her and she cringed into a tighter ball and wrapped her arms fiercely around his neck as she hid her face against him.

Lyon didn't put her down until he had her inside the backseat of his car. He quickly dragged off his raincoat and wrapped it around her. "You should hear an ambulance and fire truck any second now," he assured her. And with a tender caress of his fingers across her cheek, he was gone.

Before he reached the truck, Hope did hear sirens. The rain was easing up and the temperatures were milder than ever, but Hope hugged his raincoat closer, shivering. Shock, she realized.

She watched in dread as Lyon tried repeatedly to get Will to respond and then to drag him out, but ordinarily Will outweighed him by at least thirty pounds and in these circumstances that might as well be a hundred. As she concluded that she had to get back down there to help him, the truck turned into a fireball throwing Lyon yards back into the pasture.

Only yards down the slope, Hope froze clamping her hand against her mouth. *Dear God, no! Not Lyon, too!* she thought.

Amazingly, he scrambled to his knees and tried to reach into the truck again, but the flames forced him back—and that's what saved his life.

As firemen raced past her, two dragging a hose, another explosion flung Lyon even farther back.

Hope ran and stumbled behind EMTs to reach him. By the time she did, the EMTs were helping him up toward the street. They stopped and discreetly stepped aside and looked away as she and Lyon stared at each other. Then with a sob, Hope slumped against him. He quickly gathered her toward him, supporting her with his good arm.

"I'm sorry," he rasped.

Chapter One

The memorial service and funeral for William Jefferson Nichols II drew everyone who had ever met him or was interested in his highly publicized though short-lived pro-ball career—or was connected to the Harrells either socially, through business, or politics. With a crowd that size, the memorial service was forced to move to the high school gymnasium. Lyon had his entire department working and still had to ask for assistance from the Fannin County sheriff's department and the Texas state police.

Making things all the more challenging was the weather. Another drenching rain system was producing strong winds and adding to flood conditions. Culverts were overflowing from swelling streams and ditches making their countryside a maze of water and mud to navigate through—a challenge for locals, and a near nightmare for visiting out-of-towners in designer wear. So far, however, no deadly lightning had added to the situation, but after successfully navigating through town to the cemetery, Lyon knew better than to think they were out of the woods yet.

From his vantage point on the terrace, one block above the gravesite, he scanned the crowd below. He stood dressed in his summer uniform, the yellow rain jacket all but a fixture this week. His arms were crossed over his chest, so his right arm could serve as a rest for his bandaged left one. The tight fit of the jacket sleeve pressed on the bandages and added to the headache that had stuck with him since the night of the accident. But he couldn't complain and he had resisted the pain prescriptions written to him at the hospital. Things could have turned out much worse, and he wanted to remember that.

Only a fraction of those who'd been to the memorial service had continued over to the cemetery, but that was still too many to fit under the double tent tied to extra stakes due to the forty mph wind gusts. All four lanes surrounding the site where Will was about to join his parents, grandparents, and an aunt, created a vehicular fortress reminiscent of western movie scenes when wagon trains circled to protect the settlers from Indians. Having been born to a mother who was full Cherokee, Lyon saw the humor in that—especially since a number of these "wagons" were limousines, BMWs, Mercedes, and so forth. Lyon hadn't seen so much wealth centered in one place since Ellis had held a fundraiser for the current Texas governor.

He was doing his best to stay out of sight as much as possible and had been since the night of the accident when Rochelle Sims had burst into Emergency at Cedar Grove General and thrown her keys at him, slicing open his lower lip, which had earned him three stitches. Her subsequent tirade spread around town as quickly as the news about the wreck. As is always the case with gossip, there were a number of people willing to believe her accusations that he hadn't done enough to save Will, and by the funeral, a conspiracy theory had gained root—especially with Clyde and Mercy Nichols, Will's uncle and aunt, the closest remaining family he'd had left. There were several reasons for Clyde to show how devastated they were about Will— all of them having to do with financial profit—and so he was vowing to have Lyon's badge.

That didn't mean Lyon didn't feel some responsibility for what happened. No one could be harder on him than he was himself. If only he had made it outside of the grill in time to see it was Will behind the wheel and stopped him. While he hadn't felt a pulse when he'd reached for his old schoolmate and was fairly certain Will had broken his neck in the crash, the idea of him burning to death added to his sleeplessness. Making that all the worse was thinking how close beautiful Hope had come to dying, too. No, he wasn't going to make himself a target today for additional venting. Nevertheless, staying away hadn't been an option.

As he continued to scan the crowd, Lyon's gaze finally locked on Hope slowly working her way through a group of latecomers, thanking them for coming. She had been doing that since people had begun to arrive at the school gym almost three hours ago. Today her attire was tailored but sensible for the weather—black raincoat and tailored slacks, and boots that would have won his nod of approval if it hadn't been for the stiletto heels. She still stood out, though, among the silks and out-of-season leathers; she always did. Her other bit of fashion besides the sexy boots, was cultural, a black lace mantilla—no doubt her mother's—gracefully draped over her long black hair, the ends whipping in the wind behind her shoulders.

When the minister began to speak, she did not join Clyde and Mercy seated on the first row under the tent, unlike Ellis, who had unabashedly placed himself on their left. Instead, she stood out in the open, the wind alternately trying to push then pull her off her feet. Even from this distance Lyon noted her paleness. He fingered his radio, tempted to tell his people to get someone closer in case she needed their assistance. But knowing the audio noise would attract too much attention, upsetting her in the process, he sweated through the next few minutes, willing her to keep breathing and to stay on her feet.

Once the last prayer began, Lyon tensed. Hope started circling behind the crowd and walking toward him. With her every step, he felt a growing tightening in his abdomen as, one-by-one, people noticed her direction.

"What are you doing?" The question was whispered for his ears alone. It was pressure-relief for emotions reduced to scar tissue grown bow-tight by dread and desire for wanting the wrong woman.

Hope could have been homecoming queen, county Miss Whatever, Miss Texas and probably Miss America or Universe if that's what she'd wanted. She had what a movie producer would typecast as a smoldering sexuality, balanced by gentleness and sensitivity. What Lyon knew was that she was no stereotype and was as intelligent as anyone he knew and twice as smart as most. That made her highly attractive to ambitious men looking for more than a trophy wife. Her one weakness, however, was always siding with the underdog. Today that was apparently him.

When she stopped before him, he was unable to keep

the tenderness out of his voice or the warmth from his gaze. "Trying to earn me some loose teeth to go with this split lip?"

"I was suffocating down there. The air reeks with over-priced perfume and bad breath from money cancer." She took a deep cleansing breath. "Please don't be annoyed with me. I'm sick about what happened at the hospital, and speechless that you let Rochelle get away with it. If I'd been within hearing distance at the time, I'd have gladly decked her for you."

Lyon struggled against a choking laugh for that impossible image, as much as for her creative medical diagnosis. "I appreciate the support, Mighty Might, but you let me deal with the rabble-rousers in this town."

While his rarely-voiced pet name for her drew a smile from her, it vanished as quickly as it appeared and she was all seriousness again. "Don't joke. We need to talk."

What he needed was for her to get home and go to bed and take better care of herself than it looked like she was doing. "Not today, Hope." He nodded to the scene below. "Your father has just noticed your whereabouts."

Without bothering to glance over her shoulder, she said, "He'll recover. He has plenty going on himself not to waste time figuring out what I'm up to."

For his sanity's sake, Lyon tried a different tack. "From the itinerary we received, the Nichols' reception follows this. Aren't you expected there?"

"I'm not going. I've extended my regrets to Clyde and Mercy. I've fulfilled my obligations to them and I don't think I can stomach one more minute of him pretending he's sorry for what's happened or watching her already putting on airs. I suspect my father will skip the reception, as well—or stop by only long enough to cull the people he wants to join him at the estate for aged liquor-of-choice and illegal cigars."

"Sounds like the place to be."

Looking like she didn't believe him for a second, Hope tilted her head as she studied him and replied, "If you're into buying favors, fixing elections, and various other offensive objectives during such grim circumstances. On the other hand, I've made my mother's tortilla soup, and we both need out of this weather."

While he'd never tasted the soup, Lyon had heard enough to know Hope had inherited Rebecca Alessandro Harrell's talents in the kitchen. Add that to his unwillingness to leave her to the vultures that had been salivating over her since learning she was a free woman again and he circled the white patrol car to open the passenger door for her.

Once he was seated behind the wheel, he finally noted, "What were you doing cooking when you look like I should take you back to the hospital instead of home?"

Hardly intimidated, she replied, "You're one to talk. How's the arm?"

"Most of the bandages should come off by Monday." He knew that before they'd entered the car, she'd been eyeing his singed hair and was kind not to bring up the lingering second degree burns on the left side of his face, some third degree ones particularly on the outer shell of his ear.

"You're still a quick healer, I'm grateful."

Was she remembering when he'd suffered a concussion trying to reach his parents after the tornado that had killed them, or thinking further back to when he'd cracked a rib during a football game at the beginning of his senior year in high school and continued to play through the pain?

Either way her compassion stirred a different hunger in him and he needed relief from it.

"Could we redirect this conversation to the person who matters?" Lyon replied just as concerned. "How are you—really? I'm sorry that I haven't been around as much as I should have…as much as I intended."

"You've been inundated with job responsibilities and the press when you should have been home recuperating and avoiding infection."

Her voice was naturally soft and soothing, not quite in the second soprano range, and yet more lilting than what an alto could achieve. If she had any free time, she could easily be an in-demand voice for audiobooks; a child with a scraped knee would yearn to sit on her lap. In that way she reminded him of her mother, and his.

"Hope?"

"Yes."

"Stop. It's over. Now tell me if it was as bad as it looked?"

"Being insulated by shock helps. You lost both of your parents, you know. One operates on automatic pilot waiting for privacy to come to terms with things—in my case, too many things that should already have been dealt with. But all that aside, I know I can't pretend that what was broken could be fixed."

Hoping that she intended to expand on that, Lyon eased out of the cemetery and headed for Hope's mini-ranch, a twenty-acre oasis barely six miles south of town, three if you were traveling by crow or buzzard. Although the property was just outside of Cedar Grove city limits, Lyon passed by there often enough to know that Hope worked hard on it when she wasn't busy with her small but increasingly prestigious consulting-investment firm that also involved some social service work, as well as arranging for legal advice for landowners trying to keep their property out of greedy opportunists' hands, including her father's.

There was virtually no traffic on the road for the moment, and except for calling into the station to tell his dispatcher that he would be taking a lunch break for an hour, there were no interruptions. That made the extending silence between them palpable.

"Okay, I'll start," Hope said. "As far as I'm concerned, you should have been the one to give the eulogy."

Something good *had* come from this mess—he didn't have to. "Kent Roberts did a good job."

"Kent's been the mayor for longer than you've been chief of police and he could eulogize every dog put asleep by the animal shelter. But you were Will's best friend."

"Not lately. Not for a good while."

Hope took a deep breath. "Thank you for opening that door. Did the trouble between you two have anything to do with what I witnessed that night between him and Rochelle?"

Lyon didn't want to add to her mental anguish. "You've been through enough, Hope. And, really, what does it matter now?"

"More than you know."

He didn't care for that answer, but since she shifted her gaze out the passenger window, he took the delay—undoubtedly a temporary one—as a welcome reprieve.

When he turned into the driveway of her property, she triggered the remote she took from her purse to open the electronic gates. The property was framed in front by wrought iron and in back by ranch wire for the quarter horses she stabled there. As a child, Hope had been trained to be an equestrian rider, but quit at eighteen after the death of her mother. Some said a fall during a cross country part of a competition had caused the heart attack that had claimed Rebecca's life. In any case, five years ago, her love of horses too strong to reject, Hope turned to the western saddle form of riding. At least she stayed out of any kind of competition, Lyon thought.

Her house was a white brick hacienda-style building complete with a stucco roof. The front courtyard was framed by a cactus garden on the west, and a rose garden on the east that the house itself protected from the killer Texas sun by midday. Beyond the back fencing, he could see a vegetable garden and behind it, a peach orchard.

"You've turned this into one of the prettiest properties around," he told her driving up the concrete driveway.

"I'm glad you think so. I've been trying to talk my neighbors into letting me buy another twenty acres, but my father has been doing his best to get their whole seven-hundred acres in a lot sum, so negotiations are in limbo."

Lyon didn't understand a parent doing such a thing—especially to his only child—but Ellis was a commodity known only to himself. "It seems to me that your father has gotten progressively worse since your mother passed away."

"Only at first glance. The truth is that while she was clever and could only curb a fraction of his ego trips—as she called them—she was better at keeping his missteps and embarrassments under the gossip radar. The robber baron impulses were there all along." Hope took out another remote and triggered the third garage door. "Pull in there if you don't mind."

Under different circumstances, Lyon would hesitate. In this day of endless sex crime litigation and personality smear campaigns, no law enforcement officer, let alone city or government employee, entered a situation that even remotely seemed like a set up. But this was Hope, and Lyon knew that she was trying to protect him from gossip should his car be spotted in her driveway for longer than a minute. When the skies opened to a new deluge any hesitation became moot. As he eased the police car in, he saw her cherry red pickup was in the first garage and her black Mercedes was in the second. She always looked capable of driving either, just as she looked tantalizing whether in a formal gown or worn jeans.

Exiting the car with a smoothness and grace that belied the fact that she'd been in a life threatening accident only four days ago, Hope unlocked the door leading inside and said over her shoulder, "Make yourself at home." She led him through the washroom to the kitchen-breakfast nook area. "That door on the left is a bathroom if you need it. I'd offer you a beer or drink, but I know you'd have to turn it down. Can I get you coffee, hot tea, or a cold drink?"

After setting her purse on the nearest breakfast nook chair, she slipped off her raincoat and draped it over the back.

"Nothing, thanks." Lyon eased out of his raincoat and draped it around the chair beside hers. Adjusting some of the layers of gauze that had gotten twisted gave him time to acclimate.

Despite their mutual long friendship with Will, this was his first time here and he found the kitchen warm and welcoming, despite the cabinets being in a dark tint and the appliances black. Two significant windows—the bay window in the breakfast area that faced the courtyard and the southeast, along with a double window looking out to the patio and the west—brought in enough light without having the need for lamps unless reading or precise measuring were required.

"You've been standing for hours. Have a seat." Hope nodded to the two stools at the breakfast bar. She was rolling up the sleeves of her white pleated shirt as she made her way to the sink to wash her hands. "This won't take me any time at all."

Wondering how she'd kept track of whether he'd been sitting or not when he had only caught her looking at him once, Lyon left the first chair for her and sat on the second. Yellow and blue cushions were adorned with a Spanish design and almost matched the placemats. He also noted the accent lighting below and above cabinets, and a potted herb garden out on the back patio—all to keep his gaze off of Hope as she dried her hands and got busy. Undeniably trim, she had curves where they counted and moved like a ballerina—probably from the riding lessons she'd taken as a child, Lyon suspected.

"If the rest of the house is like this," he noted, "that explains why Will had a hard time getting you to come out to a party once you were home."

She cast him a sheepish look. "I must admit that I am something of a homebody, especially when work can keep me away from here too many hours. Confession time—I'd begun to dread the thought of having to move from here permanently."

Lyon had wondered how she and Will would work out their future living arrangements. Will would never have given up the ranch, which had been in his family for three generations. Maybe Hope had been thinking they could live part time at one residence and part time at the other, but that didn't seem practical. Then again, Will had been willing to promise her anything to get and keep his ring on her finger. That was another thing that Lyon now knew Hope hadn't been aware of.

Taking a cheerful yellow tureen from the side-by-side refrigerator, Hope set it on the bar and took two soup bowls from the cabinet beside the sink. They were also blue, yellow and white. She ladled soup into the bowls, and put the soup into the microwave to heat.

"I made beef quesadillas, too. Do you have enough of an appetite to try some?"

Lyon sat back against the sturdy oak backrest. It wasn't that he couldn't eat; he couldn't believe that with all that had happened, she had the strength and was in the frame of mind to care. "Hope…you have to quit and sit down. Preferably lie down. Remember, I'm the guy who knows too well what you've been through and I'm not above calling my doctor to come check *you* for a slow-to-show-itself injury."

"Don't threaten, Lyon. Believe it or not this is soothing and stabilizing for me. I'll warm some for us."

She took out the plate of quesadillas, plates to match the bowls, and set out napkins and silverware on the placemats. By then it was time to get out the soup and put in the rest of their meal.

Leaning over his steaming bowl, Lyon moaned in pleasure. "The accolades don't do this justice."

Hope waved him on with a potholder. "Don't wait on me, dig in."

Tempting as the encouragement was, he did wait until the rest was on the counter and she was seated beside him. Finally, he lifted the first spoonful to his lips, mindful of the stitches. After a deep-throated groan, he said, "This is better than any pain medication, and perfect for this damp-to-your-bones weather."

"I'm so glad. If you'd like, I can give you a take-home container for your dinner?"

"You won't have to offer twice. It's good to see you use black beans instead of refried stuff and that you put corn in yours," he said holding up a last bite. "My mother did, too. It's depressing how often what you get in this town is taco filling. Taco filling and refried beans masquerading as a quesadilla, taco filling as a Sloppy Joe, and taco filling as chili."

"I'll bet your mother is basking in your praise of her cooking," Hope said watching him devour the last bite and lick his fingers. "I used to buy strawberry preserves from her every year, and sweet onions. Our housekeeper could never find better."

"She told me." Lyon was glad she remembered that. He wondered if she had ever seen him watch her from the barn as she stopped at his parents' little fruit stand by the roadway in front of the farmhouse? "She said she couldn't believe anything as sweet and well-mannered as you could come from a man so twisted inside."

"No, no one will ever mistake my father for Santa Claus." Hope put down her spoon and looked straight into his eyes. "Lyon, I know you must miss your parents terribly. I still miss my mother although she's been gone years longer."

"I didn't mean to depress you further," he began.

"You aren't. But you'd make me feel much better if you promised that you aren't going to let some troublemakers chase you out of town?"

"Whoa," Lyon said slowly and eased the placemat further onto the counter so he could rest his aching arm on his good one. "That was a quick transition."

"I could tell by your eyes that you were getting impatient to know why I'd asked you here."

Lyon knew it would be a miracle in a community of less than five thousand people to avoid hearing when someone wanted your head on a platter along with your badge, but he'd hoped Hope had missed the ugly gossip nonetheless. "Not impatient," he replied. "Just concerned that something else was troubling you when you already have enough on your plate. Don't give Rochelle any more thought than she deserves."

"There are more people than Rochelle making accusations and demands," Hope replied in concern, "and you know it. I was appalled when I heard Clyde and Mercy say they agreed with her that you'd let Will die and told them so. All they had to do is look at your wounds…" Hope shook her head. "If anyone is to blame, it's me. I should have walked up to your car by myself and not allowed you to carry me. That would have given you more time to try and get Will out."

"You couldn't have walked, sweetheart. It was later determined that the truck rolled at least five times. The miracle was that you weren't killed, too, especially since the air bags didn't deploy."

Hope blinked clearly unaware of that. "They didn't, did they?"

"Your lawyer will need that information," he continued. "I can supply you with the paperwork whenever necessary."

"My lawyer—Lyon, I'm not going to sue," she replied her disbelief leaving her wide-eyed. "I wouldn't do that any more than I would blame you for Will dying." Hope swiveled her chair so that she was facing him and leaned forward to rest her elbows on her thighs so she could clasp her hands. "He had been drinking. You know that."

"That's why I'm loathe to absolve myself of all blame," he replied grimly. "If I hadn't delayed my following you outside to wait on George so I could let him know that I'd be back to monitor his locking up and escort him to the bank's night deposit, I wouldn't have missed Will grabbing the keys from you."

Hope smiled sadly. "I know. Things happen, Lyon. I was wrong for getting in the truck with him. But there were things that needed to be said."

Lyon had been haunted by the image of the empty parking slot ever since the wreck and by his imagination of how much worse things could have turned out. "If it's any consolation," he added quietly, "I'm sure Will was gone before the first explosion."

Although she closed her eyes, she nodded. "I think so, too."

Relieved that she didn't harbor any doubt, Lyon sat back in his chair slowly exhaling. "So let people say what they want. Things will calm down eventually."

Hope failed to look reassured. "Kent will stand by you, but only as long as it doesn't compromise his own political well-being. What I'm worried about is Clyde and Mercy agreeing with Rochelle, and more than that the talk of getting someone 'more dedicated' to take your place."

Wanting to make things easier for her, Lyon murmured, "I've heard what your father has been saying, Hope."

She bowed her head. "I'm so ashamed of him—he actually claims changing police chiefs would be good for the community. He means good for *his* position in the community. He just wants his own yes-man wearing your badge."

"I appreciate the concern, but if it comes to a question about the community's trust in me, I won't beg to keep the job. If trust in my work is so thin that one bombastic voice can oust someone with a proven record, then I don't want to be here."

Hope straightened, her expression growing anxious. "But we need you. You've seen how the population is growing—all that money coming from Dallas, people investing in gentlemen ranches, land prices going up when everywhere else it's a buyer's market. There's a power play going on and we need the rest of the community keeping a check on balance. I'm doing what I can, but…things have happened and I may have to cut back a bit on my pace."

Alarms went off inside Lyon. So his suspicions that she'd been avoiding him were true. Words came rushing out of him before he could stop them. "Damn it, Hope, I knew you were holding something in. What's happened? Did Will do something before the crash?"

"No. I mean it's not what you think. I'm sore, yes, but nothing else."

"Then what is it?" he demanded.

"I'm pregnant."

Thinking that she would be relieved to finally say it, Hope instead felt regret as she saw Lyon's shock, then his coloring turn ashen. His dark eyes inherited from his Cherokee mother lost all light and became like twin dark tunnels, an abyss to despair. When he covered his eyes with his uninjured hand, she felt her throat tighten with emotion. He was disappointed in her. He knew that Will had not changed and was wondering how she could stay with him, let alone get pregnant by him.

About to try to explain, she saw Lyon drag his hand down his face, rub his mouth, and clench his fingers into a fist.

"And you're telling me that you're okay?" he finally muttered. "How would you know? You left the hospital before I did having refused the tests that might have proved otherwise."

This was hardly what she expected him to say. Heartened, she impulsively touched his hand hoping to make him understand. "I needed to buy some time. I had to get through this week and today without all of the extra gossip and stares that would have occurred if I'd let them do what they would have done in ER....you know the lab results would have spread through town and points beyond faster than a Tweet."

"Are you saying Ellis doesn't even know yet?"

Hope made a ladylike scoffing sound. "If he did, that private reception at the ranch would be about buying me a husband before the family name is tarnished."

Lyon stared, incredulous. "Hope, the only one in danger of injuring your family name is the man who tries every day—Ellis himself."

She wanted to hug Lyon for completely disregarding the possibility that the baby was anyone's but Will's. His faith in her was a balm soothing her battered heart. "You're not thinking like my father does. Had I told him right away, he would be brooding over the lost opportunity of getting his hands on Nichols' property. Next on his mind, even before Will was in the ground, would be recovering some return on an asset, namely me. The fact that I'm as independent as I am constantly grates on his nerves, so he would never stand by and watch me get bloated like a beached whale without quickly trying to recoup some of his investment in me."

Veins at both of Lyon's temples grew pronounced. "Hope—that's outrageous."

The mere tip of the iceberg in her father's frozen-in-time way of thinking, she thought. "Sounds like something you're more likely to hear from the lands of lashings and stonings, isn't it? But sadly true. It wasn't too long ago that he genuinely mourned that he couldn't legally arrange a marriage for me. Mind you, I'd already been living on my own for a few years. He's entirely able and willing to try anyway. That's why I had to think things through first."

"How on earth did your mother manage to stay married to him?"

"She loved him," Hope replied with a shrug. "There were days when they barely spoke to each other, and I remember times growing up when she locked him out of their bedroom for days, but he was always allowed back in eventually. Without a doubt, the man was her Achilles' heel."

When Lyon failed to remark on that and remained silent, Hope caught on to what he must be thinking. "Yes, that's what I needed to discuss with Will and why I got into the truck with him. I told him about the baby. That's what led to the accident."

"You argued?"

"You know me better than that. But his adrenaline was flowing anyway—no doubt fueled by the alcohol. He pumped the air like a boxing champion and shouted, 'Jackpot!'"

"He said what?"

Hope nodded at his double-take. "I found that odd, too. Especially since he was responsible for protection because I was temporarily unable to continue with my birth control." Unwilling to let herself get upset again, she waved away all the negative baggage that flooded her mind like a bad dream. "Maybe that was too much information, even if the policeman is a friend," she said wryly. "I'm sorry."

"Stop that," Lyon replied. "You know that's exactly why I need to know. And as your friend I want to understand."

"Then let me get the rest out and I'll be happy not to broach the subject again." *Not even to my child when he or she is old enough to ask questions,* she promised herself. "When Will said and acted the way he did, I suddenly had a really bad feeling. I asked him if he'd tampered with the condoms." She turned to Lyon. "I was every bit as angry with what I learned as I was with what I saw when I entered the bar earlier. It turns out that he was in financial trouble and knew he might need my father's help if he couldn't repay the bank loan in time. My being pregnant was insurance to him. We were already having trouble in the faithfulness department. Correction, *he* was.

"When I heard his rationale for getting me pregnant, I told him regardless of the baby, the wedding was off. That's when I took off the engagement ring and put it in the ashtray. He got upset. He tried to make me put it back on and that's when he lost control of the truck."

In that instant Lyon looked more capable of violence than she'd ever seen him. But when he took her left hand with his right one, his touch was indescribably gentle. "If he'd hurt you more severely, I'd have ruined his pretty face for life. I'll never forgive him for what he did."

"Lyon—"

"Promise me that you'll call a doctor as soon as I leave?"

"Soon. There are a few more things that I need to resolve."

"What could be more important?" Lyon assured her, "I meant what I said. I didn't come here as a cop. Will used up my concern for him a long time ago. I came to see about you and find out what I could do to help."

"There is one thing."

"Yes, I'll drive you to the doctor. What else?"

"Marry me."

Chapter Two

Lyon's heart thudded as hard as it ever had on the football field. He was so burning mad at Will that he wasn't sure he'd heard Hope correctly at first, or was it wishful thinking? Had the big jerk survived the accident, he would have begged for the hereafter by the time Lyon finished with him.

Wherever you are, pal, you're getting off easy.

Hope was going to have a baby? His heart and stomach wrenched with dread. Granted, women did it every day and had since the beginning of time, but not Hope. She was too small, and she was virtually alone with no mother, no sister…zero close family to help in the ways that count. Fathers were useless at this stage and Ellis was ten times worse than that. Sure, she had friends…anyone with her type of accessibility and warm personality had friends. But Hope was so busy taking care of others, there wasn't much time left for enjoying her property as she deserved, let alone nurturing those relationships. Add that for all of her compassion, she was more like him—a loner who needed her private time to stay balanced—and Lyon experienced a deep-seated anxiety for her that he hadn't felt since hearing the weather reports prior to the storm a few years back that had killed his parents.

Marry me.

"You're right about your father descending on you like an F-4 tornado once he learns your condition," Lyon said finally. "But I'd only make things worse for you, Hope. You said it yourself—people have me in their crosshairs and want me gone." The irony didn't escape him in how quickly he had gone from dismissing her concerns as unlikely to a determination that she not get hurt from being too close to him.

"I think I can help make that a short-term threat. I'm a believer in the safety-in-numbers theory. There are things I can do and say to help word get out to residents who wouldn't otherwise hear about the plan to get you fired until it's too late."

"My denigrators will come after you for supporting me. How in good conscience could I allow that, particularly in your condition?"

"Maybe I can trigger a few consciences myself and people won't allow themselves to say things to me that they might to you—or the fact that I believe in you will make them wonder how true the accusations are? And who says anyone else needs to know about my condition? For the time being anyway," Hope added at his arched look.

"Are you suggesting we pass the baby off as mine?" he asked slowly.

"Maybe I'm splitting hairs, but I was thinking that if

we're not announcing a pregnancy, there's no deception. That's why I want to get a doctor out of town."

"Let me tell you the not-so-little flaw in your logic," Lyon replied, not unkindly. "There's going to be a bump where that flat tummy is now—and sooner than you think because with fate being as unkind to you as it is, that baby is going to take after Will. So much for any delay of full disclosure, unless you think it would work to suggest we'd had an affair behind his back—and you know that it wouldn't. You were about to be married to a local icon. As it is, I'd be accused of taking advantage of you while you're at your most vulnerable."

Raising her chin slightly, Hope replied, "I've been 'vulnerable' for months…if not all along. Did you catch sight of who else was at the funeral? Rochelle didn't try in the least to hide herself, and it wouldn't surprise me one bit if more of her type come out of the woodwork as time goes by." That was why she couldn't cry for Will and probably never would. He'd soiled any good memory she had of their time together and crushed any tenderness she'd held for him.

"Hope," Lyon reasoned drawing her attention back to him. "I'm not from the wrong side of the tracks, but my pedigree is nothing to the Nichols'. Marrying me is the one thing that might make your father disown you or have me murdered."

"That's not remotely funny, Lyon," Hope replied frowning. "What's more if my family's blood was ever blue, it was due to my mother." She softened her voice. "You're not going to choose now to tell me you're a reverse snob, are you?"

"What I am," he intoned, "is trying to save you from your own good intentions. You're trying to make me feel that I would be helping you as much as you would be helping me, and I just don't see it. I'd hurt you, Hope."

"No, aside from the mental pounding by my father, you'd give me protection from Clyde and Mercy."

"How so?"

"Technically Will's child would have rights to his estate, but I want them to have it."

"That alone would give your father a stroke."

"How else could I avoid them claiming visitation rights like some surrogate grandparents? I've seen enough this week to know they intend to stay close to the estate no matter who or what is in the way." Hope shook her head. "I refuse to put an innocent child into an atmosphere that makes him, or her, an obstruction."

Lyon looked torn, but when he spoke, all he said was, "When would you want to do this?"

Pressing her hand to her heart to ease the fluttering, Hope replied, "Could you check your calendar and let me know what dates you have free?"

"I'll also have to think a bit more on which explanation angle would work best for you. What if you have a blond-haired, blue-eyed baby next February or March? The nurses will panic at the first feeding time thinking there was a mistake made in the wrist banding."

He was actually going to do this, Hope thought. "My father has gray eyes and had dark blond hair before he turned gray."

Lyon cleared his throat. "People won't be thinking of your father, Hope."

"Maybe not. Or maybe by then you'll have found the love of your life and need your freedom back."

After staring at her for several seconds, he abruptly glanced at his watch that he was temporarily wearing backwards on his right wrist, and muttered an expletive under his breath. "I have to get back to the station. As good as this food is I can't handle more right now. Is that offer for a doggy bag still on?"

Although disappointed, Hope immediately went into action. "Absolutely. It won't take me a second to prepare things for you." But she wondered what had just happened. Of course he needed to get back, yet seconds ago he seemed willing to stay longer. Was it because of what she said? That understanding needed to be voiced. She didn't want him to think he couldn't be honest with her if he did meet someone. But if it happened…

As Lyon eased into his raincoat, she filled two plastic storage containers with aromatic food, then placed both in a brown bag. She couldn't deny that she was starting to get a queasy stomach—and not because of the baby.

Admit it. You don't want to think of him falling in love with anyone but you.

"These aren't throw-aways." She folded the top down on the bag. "Don't even worry about washing them. Just drop them back in the sack. Bring them anytime."

"Contrary to what you're suggesting," he replied drolly as he accepted the bag. "I'm not adverse to dishwashing detergent and water. In fact, I happen to be a decent housekeeper."

He proceeded to the door to the garage. Only when he realized that she wasn't following, did he turn around. Hope didn't have a clue as to what expression was on her face, but with a deep sigh, he retraced his steps until stopping before her.

"Forgive me," he began. "I'm admittedly tired, a little cranky and feeling way out of my comfort zone. Humor me and let me do at least one thing conventionally." Awkwardly shifting the bag into his bandaged left hand, he placed three fingers under her chin and tilted her face upwards. "Marry me?" he asked.

"Yes," she whispered.

Lyon didn't realize it hadn't stopped raining until he was a mile down the road. Uttering a self-deprecating oath, he turned on the wipers just in time to hit the brakes. He managed to miss hitting a mud-caked calf looking for dryer ground. As he and the young bovine with the guileless brown eyes studied each other, he burst into a brief but incredulous laugh. So this is what getting married was already doing to him.

Married.

He had begun to believe it would never happen. It certainly wasn't happening as he'd expected. Miraculously though, the woman was the right one.

Hope's face when he kissed the corner of her mouth would be imbedded in his memory forever. Hope in Hope's eyes was a mesmerizing thing. There was no denying that he'd wanted a different kiss, but he needed to be patient. He would be. Look what it had done for him so far.

Mind back on the job, he directed himself as he eased around the indecisive calf. The need to return to the station was real enough, but he'd had to get the devil out of there because of Hope's generous commitment to null and void their contract if "he met the love of his life." That had stung more than he could deal with in her presence because he didn't want to believe she could do it. If matters were reversed, there was no way in hell he could step back politely and say, "Okay, bye."

Back at the station he was greeted by the dispatcher, Buddy Yantis, who was the only one there at the moment.

The rest of the department was either taking lunch, or returning home until their night shift began, except for their one full-time detective, Cooper Jones, who was in court today. Despite the mild temperatures, Buddy was sweating and mopping his high forehead and balding head with a Dairy Queen napkin taken from around his Blizzard cup that one of the other officers must've dropped off. Usually calm and collected, that told Lyon that they had problems.

"What's happened?" he asked.

"Mr. Harrell." Buddy's hands shook as he held up three pink phone messages. "He expects you to call."

"I'm sure he does." Lyon took the slips of paper and nodded toward the door. "Take ninety minutes and go see your wife and baby."

"I'm okay, Chief. I can wait until I'm relieved."

Buddy was a war vet. He'd been serving in Iraq when a roadside bomb killed the three other soldiers in his armored vehicle and delivered a concussion so severe to Buddy that he was given a medical discharge. Several other police departments had rejected his application for employment, but Lyon had seen the desperation of a husband and father trying to rebuild his life and offered him the dispatcher's position on a trial basis. The last five months had been going well, until today.

"Yes, you could," Lyon replied calmly. "But you don't have to. I'll be fine until some of the others return. Don't let me see you back here until—" he checked his watch "—two o'clock. Understood?"

Buddy's bloodshot, green eyes grew bright with relief and gratitude. "Thank you, sir." He was out of the building faster than hurrying to a muster call.

Detouring to the break room, Lyon grabbed a pen from

the lunch table and wrote his name on the bag. Then he put his food from Hope into the full-size refrigerator. All the while he was thinking about Ellis and what the insensitive tyrant might have said to leave Buddy a step away from a mandatory visit to his VA psychiatrist. No wonder Hope's phone hadn't rung while he'd been at her house. Ellis had been having too much fun intimidating the least deserving person in his department.

Once in his office, Lyon took his time to check the rest of his messages. Then he downloaded his computer's Inbox. He sent notes of thanks to liaisons with the state police and county offices, and only then dialed Ellis' phone number.

"Harrell residence," a clipped voice announced.

"Chief Teague," Lyon replied. "I'm returning Mr. Harrell's call."

"I'll see if he's in, sir."

Lyon heard raucous laughter and male voices in the background. The party Hope had mentioned must be in full swing, he thought.

"Took your damned time," Ellis snapped instead of a greeting. "Did that idiot tell you that I called multiple times?"

"I have all of Officer Yantis' message slips in front of me, Mr. Harrell," Lyon replied mentally gritting his teeth. "And for the record, Buddy Yantis is a decorated war veteran. I'd appreciate you give him the same respect that he undoubtedly gave you. Now what seems to be your problem?"

"Where's my daughter?"

"At home."

"You drove her?"

"I did."

"I called there several times. I got no answer."

"Maybe she took her doctor's advice and pulled the

plugs to get some rest." Lyon could only hope that she did, but maybe her old man was bluffing. The phone hadn't rung while he was at Hope's.

After a weighty silence, Ellis said, "Let's cut through the sweet talk. I don't know what you're up to, but stay away from her."

"Excuse me?"

"You heard me. She's not herself right now and I won't have you taking advantage."

"Anything else?" Lyon asked keeping his tone flat.

"Yes. I want your badge. The more you annoy me, the sooner I'll get it."

"I had no idea you've filed for mayor," Lyon drawled.

Ellis slammed down the phone.

"By all means," Lyon murmured. Replacing the receiver in the phone's cradle, Lyon crushed the pink slips and dropped them into the trash can behind his chair. "Give it your best shot."

Not only did Hope lie down after Lyon left, totally exhausted and relieved, she slept until a mockingbird outside her bedroom window started its repertoire of impersonations at three in the morning. With almost fourteen hours of sleep to help her recuperate she soon made her way to the kitchen where she started a pot of coffee. She knew she wouldn't be able to go back to bed now that her mind had cranked into gear. Besides, there was plenty to do. She was checking the water in almost a dozen bouquets and that many potted plants scattered around the house—delivered since word got out about Will's passing—when the ringing phone startled her. Hope spilled a bit of water setting down the copper can and returned to dry off the antique oak chest with the remote to her ear. "Yes?"

"So you are awake. I saw the lights on and wondered if something was wrong, or you just didn't want to sleep in the dark?"

Hope immediately went to the breakfast nook bay window and angled to see the street. There she saw head-lights at the front gate. Her heart did a little skitter at the thought that Lyon was this concerned about her. "Hang on, I'm letting you in." Dashing to the garage, she also pressed the third door's button to open that for him, as well.

When Lyon untangled his long limbs from the car, Hope saw that he looked bleary-eyed and his hair was more than singed, it was rumpled from either tossing and turning instead of sleeping, or else raking his hand through it too often. Blood-shot eyes aside, his low-hooded caressing gaze made her feel a little underdressed in her white sports bra and shorts. She had been intending to work out to a yoga video right after she finished watering.

"You look like you need eyedrops as much as coffee," she said as she stepped back to let him enter.

"Too much paperwork to catch up on." Reaching the kitchen he sniffed the air and moaned. "Feel free to admin-ister that through an IV."

"It will be ready in two minutes," Hope said closing up after him. "Don't tell me that you haven't even been to bed yet?" While he didn't have a pronounced beard, it was obvious that he had shaved recently.

"I tried, but I gave up wrestling with the bed sheets."

"Oh, dear. And am I the cause of your unrest?"

"No, my other fiancée." Although his gaze was admiring, and he brushed a tender kiss on her cheek, he raised his eyebrows at her attire. "Please tell me that you weren't planning to head outside to jog?"

"Heavens, no. Yoga. I try to get in at least fifteen minutes most mornings and thirty on weekends. It's a wonderful stress reliever."

"That explains those fluid limbs and how you move like a dancer. You definitely look more rested than when I left you." He pulled out the same barstool and sat down.

"I wish I could return the compliment. Are you hungry? I can make you a skillet breakfast."

"Just coffee, thanks. I indulged myself with the rest of your lunch while watching the ten o'clock news. The bag with the containers is on the passenger seat. Don't let me forget to give it to you."

"Okay." Hope got another mug and set it before him on the placemat. It was a man's mug—big with a handle designed for man-sized hands, and no flowers, unlike her delicate sunflower one. When she poured the coffee and the aromatic brew wafted up to his nostrils, he closed his eyes and inhaled with appreciation.

"Lyon, I'm sorry that I'm giving you such a headache," Hope said filling her own mug. "Is this where you tell me that you've changed your mind?"

When he didn't answer right away, it was impossible for Hope to even think of tasting her own stabilizing but hot brew. Her heart tanked. After that sweet kiss, she'd assumed—well, hoped—that he would immediately reassure her.

"What I need," he said finally meeting her pensive gaze, "are some clarifications."

"About…?"

"How you expect this arrangement to work? I mean

technically we'll be entering into a marriage of convenience, only you have to admit it's going to be anything but convenient."

She understood. At least she thought she did. He was referring to this complicating his love life, even though he'd told her that presently there was no special someone. That didn't necessarily mean that he was celibate. But how could she give him her blessing to do what he needed to do when the mere thought nearly made the coffee she'd just swallowed rise back up her throat?

"Hope, what I'm asking is, you are wanting us to live together, right?"

"Well, we'll be living and working in the same town, so unlike some bi-coastal couples, I can't see a way around it," she replied curling the end of her ponytail around her right index finger. "It's not going to appear all that convincing if you stay in that apartment while I'm over here." She knew that he lived in the two-story string of rentals three properties behind the police and volunteer fire stations.

Although he narrowed his eyes, the corners of his mouth twitched. "I was trying to be a gentleman and wait for you to invite me."

She hadn't actually done that, had she? They'd parted with so much yet to discuss, no wonder he couldn't get any rest. "You'd be doing me another huge favor and bringing me great peace of mind if you'd agree to live here, Lyon," she recited. Then she worried. "It's not too far from the station, is it? You're welcome to share my office. We might have to rearrange things if you have a lot of equipment."

"The distance isn't a problem and the only office stuff I have is a laptop and a four-drawer file cabinet. I tend to do my work at the kitchen bar, so you don't have to worry about being cramped at your desk. On the other hand if your guestroom is already furnished, I'll probably need to put my other stuff in storage."

Hope marveled at how he'd handled their sleeping arrangements so matter-of-factly. But in the next instant, she felt dejected that he hadn't needed clarification on *that*. Had she been way off on her hunch that he was sexually attracted to her?

"The room is furnished," she said determined to sound as normal as he did, "but there's no need for you to waste money on a storage unit. As you've probably noticed, there's plenty of room in the garage."

"You're sure? The money isn't an issue, but the amount of wildlife that often inhabits those places could considerably shorten the lifespan of my things."

"I'm sure."

Lyon took another sip of coffee. "All right then, how about your cleaning lady? Can she be trusted not to spread stories around town about us?"

Startled, Hope asked, "How did you know about Molly?"

"I met her in town one day when a couple of punks were taunting her as she tried to get into her pickup truck over by the farm and ranch supply store. They parked too close and she couldn't open her door. They wouldn't move. After I had a few words with them, I made sure she was okay. That's when I learned who she was and where she worked."

"Molly never said anything about that."

"She probably didn't want to upset you," Lyon replied. "She seems a sweet lady."

"Oh, she is. And as you probably surmised, she's not exactly like most people."

"Was she born that way or did an accident injure her mental state?"

Once again Hope was touched by the considerate way he posed his question. "When she was younger and living in Mississippi, she had an abusive boyfriend. That's how her husband Tan met her. He said the guy kicked her out of his moving car on a bridge. She not only hit the pavement, but fractured her skull on the iron bridge beams."

"Tan?"

Gesturing behind her toward the back acres, Hope replied, "Tan Lee. He works for me, too. He witnessed the crime and testified in court on her behalf. In fact, he'd seen her earlier in the day at a farmer's market. You might say that he fell in love on sight. When he saw what a jerk her boyfriend was, he was worried for her safety and followed them. I understand that he visited her in the hospital every day until her release."

"I think I've seen him a few times. Asian? Mid to late thirties?"

"Vietnamese. And, yes, he's about twelve years her senior, but that seems to have worked for them." She gestured toward the back again. "You haven't seen all of the property, but I put a camper by the pond in the northwest corner. I hope to build them a cottage by next year. Molly helps me with the housework and gardening. Tan is living his dream to be a cowboy on a Texas ranch—small though it is. He's doing beautifully with the horses when he's not costing me a small fortune in diesel fuel on the tractor. It appears that the one thing he likes more than animals is all things mechanical."

"Hope's Shelter for the Abused and Chronic Dreamers," Lyon murmured.

She gave a philosophical nod and shrug. "Guilty. At least you're kinder than my father about it. But they really have helped me more than whatever I've managed to do for them. To answer your question, though, both Tan and Molly rarely go to town except to run an occasional errand when I can't do something myself, and you'll find them too protective of me to gossip. Truth be told, Tan struggled to hide his dislike for Will. Having them here would have been the only good thing about having to move. I would have been able to keep this place and trust them to maintain things."

Lyon grimaced. "No telling how leery they'll be of me invading the place so out of the blue."

"They already know you saved my life," Hope said eager to assure him. "They're going to think you're as wonderful as I do."

The look she received for that had Hope all but weak-kneed. To keep from making a fool of herself, she spun away to grab the coffeepot and topped off both of their mugs.

"Are you telling them about the baby?" Lyon asked.

"It's the wise thing to do. Anything could happen—I could fall or have an accident…or something could go wrong early in the pregnancy. They need to know to get me help if I'm in no condition to do it myself."

"And to find me immediately."

Hope returned the pot to the machine and wrapped her arms around herself. His concern touched her deeply and his brushed-suede voice caressed her in places it was safer not to think about. "Thank you, Lyon."

"Can we talk like this if we cross paths in town?"

"As long as you resist offering to shake my hand," she quipped.

The mug was halted midway to his mouth. "Now when did I ever do that?"

"I'm teasing. At any rate, you've always been welcoming and make people feel like there's no one else you'd rather speak with."

"We're not talking about people," he replied with some weariness, "we're talking about—maybe I should get you an engagement ring."

"No! Oh, no," she said less anxiously. "Please don't go through that expense. What I would really like is a wedding band, not too wide, maybe with some delicate scrolling, nothing with stones, nothing square or rectangular so that there are edges. I don't want to constantly worry that a gem has come loose and been lost, or to keep getting hung on my clothes or scratching furniture."

Lyon frowned. "You're not saying that to protect my wallet or pride, are you? I may not have Will's bankroll, Hope, but that hardly makes me destitute."

"I'm not comparing. Besides, I told you Will wasn't as financially flush as he led everyone to believe. He was real estate rich, but cash poor. That ring he gave me was all for show. If it's ever found, it needs to go to Clyde and Mercy. They may need it to cover back taxes or who knows what else."

"That's extremely decent of you."

"It's the right thing to do."

"Well, I can tell you from what I've seen of relationships that have gone south, not every woman would share your perspective." Eyeing her hands as she toyed with her hair again, he relented. "A band it is. We could stop somewhere and look at some when we go for the license. I'd like one myself."

"Would you?" Hope couldn't hide her surprise and delight. "Why Lyon—thank you!"

Suddenly he looked less tired and far more pleased with himself. "I did check my schedule...what do you think about next Thursday?"

"That will work, provided we don't leave until afternoon. I have a consultation in the morning that could take a while. An elderly woman who was recently widowed. She knows nothing about her finances because her husband had always managed everything."

"Well, she's in good hands now," Lyon said.

"Would you mind us going down to Rockwall for the license? It's far enough away that we shouldn't run into anyone from here, and they have a nice historic courthouse. Lake Ray Hubbard makes for a scenic background, too." Just north of downtown Dallas in the last several years the area had mushroomed into its own not-so-little enclave of shops and restaurants, while elegant homes and condominiums lined the lake. "I know this is a marriage of convenience," she said wistfully, "but that doesn't mean we can't make the day enjoyable, even special."

His gaze dropped briefly to her lips. "We'll make it whatever you want it to be."

Heaven help her, Hope thought. Practically everything he was saying was rocketing her imagination into forbidden territory.

"This is all falling into place almost too easily," Hope murmured. "Lyon, I can't tell you how grateful I am for how agreeable *you're* being." To her surprise he not only dropped his gaze, his expression seemed guilty.

"You may take that back when I tell you that your father called me today," he said.

"Oh." Was that the real reason he couldn't sleep? Once again she wrestled with disappointment and guilt. Guilt won. Harrells were turning his world upside down and inside out. "I expected his first line of attack would be me and that my phone would be ringing off the wall," she said while wondering what Ellis had up his sleeve. "But it never did."

"He said he tried to reach you several times."

She shook her head slowly and went to the kitchen phone. Lifting the remote, she clicked the green icon, heard the dial tone and clicked on the red. Returning the remote to its cradle, she asked, "What did he have to say?"

"Nothing you haven't already heard or can't imagine. After warning me to stay away from you, he came right out and declared he was coming after my badge."

"At least now you believe me that he's serious."

"I believed you all along, Hope. I simply didn't want you worrying about me when you had enough going on."

"But can you see that my support of you will help thwart his plans and this proves he thinks so, too?"

"Maybe."

Hope accepted that.

"One thing," he continued, "and this isn't a negotiable issue. When you tell your father about us, I want to be there."

"But that will only encourage him to be all the more unpleasant. That's so unfair to you."

"How so if I'm half the man you make me out to be? We may not share a bed, Hope, but we'll be sharing vows. The responsibility that comes with them began when I agreed to this."

She had long thought him a principled and honorable man, but her respect and feelings deepened tenfold with that pronouncement. Coming at the end of a week of emotional upheaval and psychological turmoil, her throat tightened, her eyes burned with unshed tears. She wished she could articulate what she was feeling. Carrying the child of a man she had stayed with longer than she'd loved him left her with a sense of dues to pay and wrongs to be righted. But she ached for how things could have been if she'd made different choices sooner. All she could do was try to get it right from now on.

"All right," she replied. "We'll face him together."

Chapter Three

As planned, on the following Thursday, Lyon and Hope drove down to Rockwall, the county seat of Rockwall County, which claimed the distinction of being the smallest county in Texas. It turned out that it was closer to three in the afternoon before they could get away.

With the sun nudging temperatures into the eighties and the medians along the north corridor of Interstate 30 changing from a flood of Indian paintbrush and crimson clover to summer wildflowers like black-eyed Susans and butterfly weeds, it was a perfect afternoon to be on the road. Hope had suggested they use her Mercedes for the trip and was glad when Lyon hesitated only briefly. Using his patrol car was a non-option, and their pickup trucks might still be considered the real Cadillacs by Texans, but neither would provide the right tone for this trip.

After a few years of seeing Lyon always in his uniform,

Hope couldn't help but admire him in his camel blazer, white dress shirt, and jeans. His black dress boots were polished to a military shine. She was relieved for him that his burns healed as fast as he'd assured her they would and that the doctors had let him remove the bandages on his left arm. He admitted his arm remained a bit stiff and the new skin felt a little tight, but it looked as though in time the scarring would be minimal. Yesterday's trip to his barber had eradicated most of the damage to his hair.

"You look like a very tough marine about to be deployed," she told him.

"I look scalped," he muttered.

Coming from him that was almost amusing, except that it made her think of how much worse things could have gotten. Grateful, Hope lifted her face to the warming sun. With the moon roof slightly open, her hair, feathered around her face, tickling her now and again, and she smiled feeling better than she had for some time.

She had chosen to wear a powder blue sheath topped with a matching bolero jacket trimmed with coffee brown lace. The lace collar stood up like gowns from the Elizabethan period and ruffled at her wrists. The earrings she brushed against as she smoothed her hair were turquoise in a squash-blossom design—another inheritance from her mother. She'd worn them and the delicate matching cross necklace hoping to feel her spirit—and she did.

"Where did you go just now to put that lovely, serene smile on your face?" Lyon asked.

"I was just thinking of my mother—and thank you."

"Would Miss Rebecca have approved of what her only child was doing?"

Hope considered the question for a few seconds. "She

would have worried, maybe, but understood. At any rate, what could she say considering who *she* married?"

"Good point."

"Then again, if she was still here, this wouldn't be necessary. She would have taken her riding crop to my father."

"And banished him from the bedroom."

"Exactly," she laughed.

After passing a USPS truck towing two trailers, Lyon continued. "Did you warn Tan and Molly that it might be dark before we get back?"

"Yes, Chief, *and* they have my cell phone number." At his sidelong look, she added, "It's all right, Lyon. I've been out after dark before."

"But you've never been pregnant before."

That was becoming his favorite mantra. Their engagement had tripped a protective switch in him, not that she really minded. She was also seeing how much more attentive Tan was growing since learning she was expecting. Suddenly, she couldn't get near the horses without him shadowing her, and now he insisted on unloading feed bags by himself. Molly was almost as bad; Hope could no longer carry anything heavier than a laundry basket. Climbing the kitchen ladder to dust the tops of cabinets and refrigerator was an invitation to hear Molly hum off key—a quirk she'd developed to help her cope when she became stressed.

"I have a feeling you're all going to get pretty annoying by the time I'm in maternity clothes," she told Lyon.

"Doesn't hurt for you to be the one being spoiled for a change. You do that plenty enough for others."

"Ah-ha…so being bird-dogged and shadowed is a gift."

It was a relief to see him relaxed and enjoying the drive,

as much as she was. The last several days had tested his resilience and commitment to the job.

On Monday, a "name withheld" Letter to the Editor had appeared in their weekly newspaper accusing Lyon of having something other than coffee in his mug at the grill the night of the accident. By Tuesday, rumor had it that seventy-five more people had signed the petition to terminate Lyon's contract with the city. Outraged, George Bauman, the grill's owner and bartender, had stormed into the newspaper's office and called Ted Pettigrew, owner and editor-in-chief of the *Cedar Grove Chronicle,* an enabler and idiot for allowing such libelous garbage to be printed and pulled his standing ad. But Ted remained unapologetic. He loved conflict wherever he could find it or stir it up, and gleefully informed George that he had two more letters critical of Lyon waiting for next week's issue.

Perhaps the most disturbing and disappointing occurrence was that one of Lyon's youngest officers, Chris Sealy, told him that his wife wanted him to quit and move to another town and police department because she "worried for his safety under Chief Teague." The embarrassed young officer acknowledged that his wife's cousin was Rochelle and that she thought she owed Rochelle her support. Nothing was set in stone yet, but it appeared Lyon would be looking for a new police officer before long.

That wasn't to say there weren't pleasant surprises to emerge like intermittent sunshine between storm clouds. Hope was learning that Lyon liked to call at least twice a day to see what she was up to—three times if he couldn't meet her for lunch or when a planned dinner together wouldn't work out. And so far they had only shared one dinner due to him trying to work ahead so that he could take a few extra days off to move once they were married.

As for her father, Hope had declined two of his dinner invitations. She'd cited her workload as her excuse. On a hunch, though, she'd driven past the ranch on the night of the first invitation and, sure enough, spotted Clyde and Mercy's aging Lincoln Towncar in the driveway. That made turning down the second invitation easier.

Before they reached Greenville, Hope winced and slipped out of the designer heels that matched the lace on her dress. "The Internet tells me that this embryo is the size of a pin head, but I've already gained two pounds and I think it's all in my feet! With my luck, I'll be wearing an NBA size by the time I deliver."

"What are you doing wearing shoes not broken in yet?"

"These aren't new, cowboy. I'm not so foolish and fashion crazy as to wear new shoes when I know I'll be on my feet for hours…but they are a half-inch higher than what I usually wear."

"No, not fashion crazy at all," Lyon drawled.

"Yes, you guys *hate* that we try to look our best for you."

"Can't stand it," he said agreeably. "By the way, what do you call that nail polish?"

"Iced Mocha." She wiggled her toes delighted that he'd noticed.

"That was my first guess, too." By now Lyon was almost sporting dimples. "What size shoe are you, a six?"

"Lucky guess."

"That's why they pay me the big bucks they do."

Leaning her head back against the seat, Hope studied him openly. "Lyon, why haven't you ever married?" It was a question she'd wondered about often, all the way back to when Will had suggested she play matchmaker for his buddy. But she'd never been satisfied with any of the potential partners Will had suggested.

When Lyon didn't answer, she waved away the question. "Forget that. I shouldn't have gotten that personal."

"We're about to live under the same roof. Something tells me we'll be hard-pressed to avoid getting more personal. Only...can I give you a rain check?"

"Sure, I'll be around," she quipped. But it wasn't all right and Hope immediately started speculating. Was he pining over someone? In a town their size, it was fairly easy to remember whom he'd dated and the ones who hadn't moved away appeared to be happily married. Had someone left Cedar Grove that she had forgotten about?

"Don't burn valuable brain cells."

Caught in the act, Hope stiffened to keep from squirming. "I'm not. I was about to ask how things went in court the other day? You never did say." Instead they had talked about the challenge of finding packing boxes and the most opportune time to transport them to an apartment when you weren't ready to tell anyone you were moving, or seem to confirm that an employment switch was looming.

"It turned out that I wasn't needed after all. I sat in the hall for two hours—the second lunch we missed—and then the guy accepted the plea bargain. He's already down in Huntsville. I'd rather talk about what you'd like to do after we get the license and rings. Dinner overlooking the lake might be nice. In fact I took a chance and made reservations at the Hilton."

Hope gasped with surprise and delight. Although there were some fun places with good food opening around the huge Bass Pro shop on the east side of the Interstate, the

Hilton provided more elegant, gourmet dining. *"Mistra's?"*

"I booked us for six o'clock. I hope that I left enough time to shop for the rings."

Hope couldn't believe he'd done this—actually wanted somewhere more formal. "I love that place. Have you been there before?"

"No, but I found it online. It seemed to suit you more than anything else I saw."

That was high flattery coming from a man who didn't seem to say anything that he didn't mean. "When I have a meeting with anyone in or around the city, I try to book it there. Not only does it split the driving distance, but the ambiance eases the tedium of talking numbers and growth patterns. It reminds me of Greece and the Mediterranean— open and airy, sun-bleached whites and cerulean blues. In fact that's where it gets its name."

"I wondered—or if it was named after the owner or chef?"

"No, for centuries, Mistra was a fortified city with quite a reputation for culture and philosophy."

"Have you been to Greece?" Lyon asked.

"Years ago, but not to the island, and I was quite young, so much of the art and history was wasted on me, but it's where I learned to love goat cheese—and probably cost my mother months off her life while diving from the cliffs. I really appreciate this, Lyon."

The courthouse was busy, but they waited their turn to fill out the application and then sat dutifully before the clerk and finished the paperwork. In less than forty minutes they were back outside, but that left them with the minimum time for ring shopping before their dinner reservations.

The first jewelry store had a beautiful selection, but

despite Lyon's coaxing, Hope held to her request for something simpler. The next store had a pair of bands they both liked and the inventory was such that they walked out with the small bag containing the symbols of their future.

At the hotel, they left the Mercedes with the valet and proceeded to the restaurant. As soon as the maître d' spotted her, his expression of cool reserve warmed to a wide smile. "Ms. Harrell! What a pleasure. I didn't realize you'd be a guest this evening."

"Thank you, Ivo. It's always good to see you."

"I would have thought we wouldn't be having the pleasure of your company for some time. My deepest sympathies for your loss."

Hope felt Lyon shift closer behind her and his hand go immediately to her waist. She appreciated that since she had completely overlooked that anyone here would have seen the obituaries, which was foolish of her. "I appreciate that so much," she replied. She stepped aside to gesture to Lyon. "This is Chief of Police Teague from my town. Lyon, Ivo Martini."

"Ah! Chief Teague, yes, we have the reservation. An honor, sir." With a bow he quickly stopped the hostess who was assigning a table and with a discreet few words did some hasty rearranging of her seating chart. "Please follow me," he said with menus in hand, then led them to the circular part of the restaurant where floor-to-ceiling windows looked out onto the pool and beyond it the lake.

"The best seats. You're already spoiling us, Ivo." Hope eased onto the chair that he held out for her.

"We will all do our best." He opened her leather menu and handed it to her and then did the same for Lyon. "We're featuring wines from South Africa this week."

"Thank you, but I can't this visit," she told him. "I'll just have water, thank you."

"I'll keep her company," Lyon said.

The slender man bowed again. "Medication, of course. I should have known better. But you look wonderful, Ms. Harrell. It's a blessing to still have you with us. I'll tell Martin and he will get your drinks and take your order. Enjoy."

"Amen to the blessing part," Lyon murmured once the dignified man was out of earshot.

Hope leaned toward him, distressed. "Lyon, I should have known he would have seen the papers. *The Dallas Morning News* did a sizable story on Will. I'm sorry that I didn't think to warn you as soon as you told me about the reservations."

"Never mind me, are you all right with this? It can't be comfortable. We can leave."

"No. I wouldn't do that to you and it wouldn't be fair to Ivo and the others." She just needed to keep her wits about her and not look too happy to be there with him.

"There you go thinking of everyone but yourself again. I hate that you won't relax now and enjoy yourself as you should have."

"We have the license, the rings, and we'll have a delicious dinner. Our cup pretty much runs over."

"Did Will ever come here with you?"

Having anticipated that question would be asked at some point, Hope realized that she didn't want to deceive him. "We stopped for drinks once on our way back from a Cowboy game. They were playing his old team and Will was eager to extend the night as long as he could to celebrate the win he had nothing to do with. Needless to say, I drove us the rest of the way home and never brought him again. Ivo was kind to forgive me."

"You have a distinct fan in him."

"The affection is mutual."

Lyon lowered his gaze to the menu. "So if we're staying, what do you recommend?"

After some discussion, Lyon ordered the warm Texas Gulf shrimp cocktail for an appetizer, while she revisited the corn-crusted scallops and oysters on a stand fork with grain mustard *mousseline*. Next Lyon chose the house salad, although he was skeptical about what the *manchego* cheese was and whether he would like the sweet sherry vinegar-mango dressing.

"That's Spanish cheese, made from sheep's milk instead of cows'," Hope told him. When his expression grew wary, she coaxed, "A former farm boy can handle that."

"I could handle a wedge of iceberg lettuce doused with Thousand Island dressing topped by a couple of cherry tomatoes, too."

Hope chose the baby spinach with Roquefort dressing, spiced pecans and strawberries. Lyon discreetly begged some of the pecans and she shared but wished she could have fed them to him with her fork. So much for the fantasy of a romantic pre-wedding dinner.

For their entree Lyon ordered the New York strip, while she had the lamb T-bone. Her meat was so thick she ended up giving him the entire rib portion and kept only the fillet.

"Just don't go around telling everyone back home that I prefer lamb to beef," Lyon warned when she looked too tickled at how quickly he'd devoured his food. "If those cattle ranchers hear that, you and the Four Horsemen won't be able to keep them from running me out of town."

"Until here, the best I've ever tasted was in *The Pink Adobe* in Santa Fe," she told him. "I remember it was served with acorn squash and a black cherry sauce." Here they'd served spinach and a goat cheese stack.

"My mother would have liked that. She used all of the squashes."

"I'll attempt to duplicate it for you when the weather cools."

The look he sent her left her as warm as the chiminea did that night, but the sense of being closely observed by the staff compelled Hope to keep her expression benign, and she and Lyon stuck to impersonal subjects after that—or remained silent when anyone was within hearing distance. The strain took its toll and Hope passed on dessert when Lyon asked what she would like. "If you don't mind," she added.

"Not at all," he replied before the waiter could reach them. "I'm ready to go, too. As lovely as you look framed by these surroundings, I prefer the company of the woman who took her shoes off in the car."

Hope coughed discreetly into her linen napkin to cover a chuckle. But once they were in the Mercedes and Lyon was pulling away from the valet station, she voiced her true feelings.

"Did you at least enjoy the food? I'm so sorry this wasn't the dinner you wanted for us."

"The food was terrific and any time spent with you can't be a disappointment," he assured her.

How different he was from Will, she thought, although she disliked herself when she made comparisons. But Will's compliments tended to become like cold cream—a little too thick, while Lyon's she could accept with pleasure and not feel them linger uncomfortably between them. In fact, they weren't on the Interstate but a minute or two when she not only slipped out of her shoes, she was struggling to stay awake.

"This is crazy," she said after stifling a series of yawns. "I've had no alcohol or sugar. Why am I about to fall asleep?"

"I can think of a few reasons, not counting that you have a little package inside you gobbling up half of your energy. You'd better make that doctor's appointment soon and ask what vitamins you need."

"That's next on the list after the wedding."

"All the more reason to bump up the wedding. How does Tuesday sound for you?" At her startled glance, Lyon shrugged. "I have court on Monday, but it should be a one-day situation. Tuesday is free appointment-wise. I can either call a justice of the peace in Sherman or Gainesville. Both are sometime poker pals and would protect our privacy."

"Sherman," she replied without hesitation. "That's closer and we can get back sooner and have a celebratory dinner at the house."

"That's not fair, you cooking on your wedding day— even if it isn't a normal wedding."

"I told you, as much as I appreciate a good meal out on occasion, I'm a homebody at heart. I can prepare a few things in advance and you can grill the steaks in back while I finish up."

"That sounds better. I'll pick up the steaks over the weekend—and bring a suitcase with what I'll need to change into before we head off to Sherman."

"Perfect."

That was the last thing Hope remembered saying to him. The next thing she knew, she felt a warm caress on her cheek. When she opened her eyes, Lyon was leaning over and releasing her seat belt.

"You'll be more comfortable in your bed than spending the night in this car," he told her.

She glanced around and saw they were in her garage. All that time and noise of opening and shutting doors, too! "Good grief, Lyon! You shouldn't have let me sleep the whole way."

"I didn't mind. I'm glad you felt comfortable enough to sleep around me."

He was too dear to turn her rude behavior into a compliment. "Would you like to come in for a cup of coffee...or drink now that you're so close to home?" she asked as she got out and searched in her purse for her keys.

Lyon beat her to it using the keys she'd already given him, just as he'd used his own gate and garage door openers. "No thanks, I'm good. But if you don't mind, I'd like to make sure everything in the house is okay."

Hope didn't mind at all. She'd confessed that she didn't use her security system now that she had Tan and Molly around. Molly could forget about the alarm and it had upset her greatly once when she walked in and forgot how to turn it off. Although she could rely on Tan to keep an eye on the house during the day, by now he and Molly were in bed.

By the time he returned, Hope had placed her purse and shoes in her room and left her jacket on the chair by the closet. He took the small jeweler's bag from his pocket and set it on the kitchen counter.

"It's probably safer here than in an apartment that I'm rarely at," he said.

"I'll put it in the safe," she replied. "You're sure I can't get you anything?"

"A good-night kiss—and then you'd better get to bed before you fall asleep again this time while standing up."

When he lowered his head, clearly intending to kiss her cheek, Hope turned her head so that his lips met hers. His eyes opened and looked into hers, and then he slowly kissed her again. His lips grew firmer against hers and Hope felt something like champagne bubbles rush through her veins.

"Sweet dreams," he murmured against her lips.

"You, too."

When he closed the door quietly behind him, Hope leaned against the counter and covered her flat tummy with her hands. "Oh, baby," she whispered. "That was all the dessert Mommy needed."

On their wedding day, Lyon woke instantly alert and wishing it was already afternoon. When he'd called Ed Viney over in Sherman last Friday morning, the justice of the peace had enthusiastically said, "Marry you to Harrell's girl? And he doesn't know? Get over here! That'll be such a treat, I'm waiving my fee."

The support was more than welcome considering that Ellis had tried to get Hope over to the ranch on Saturday night to play hostess for what he described as a "friendly little dinner party." It turned out that one of the guests was to be Jack Nolan, who just happened to be one of Austin's most eligible bachelors. Hope declined and Lyon—having brought over that suitcase and several boxes of his things—got to hear Ellis' volcanic response even from several feet away. He'd known Ellis had a temper but never imagined he would treat a daughter and only child that way. It was all he could do not to take the phone from Hope and give the big bully a long overdue scare. In fact, Hope moved to the other side of the kitchen bar to make sure he didn't.

"Next time you suspect this wedding is only to help you

keep your job, remember that call," she told him after hanging up. "I know Jack Nolan a bit, and he would be like Will—placate my father to avoid the tirades."

Lyon looked from the phone back to her taking a moment to keep the fury out of his voice. "Once you're wearing my ring, I'd better not hear him tearing you like that again, or he'll be cooling off in a holding cell."

"You couldn't arrest him for bellowing like one of his cranky bulls," she replied with some anxiety.

"You're pregnant," he reminded her again. "You're carrying his grandchild. Would you have me wait for you to miscarry?"

After that call, a herd of feral hogs couldn't force him to leave her except when she was ready to turn in for the night. Hope made them a pizza from scratch, which they ate outside on the patio watching hummingbirds do dive-bomber acrobatics as they tried to claim one of the four feeders as their very own. Later they walked the twenty acres, chatted with Tan and Molly, and treated the horses to slices of apple. Lyon hadn't felt so content and aware of spring's promise since he was waiting for his high school senior year to start—and getting his driver's license and first car.

And now it was Tuesday and he was about to take himself a wife. He liked the old fashioned phrasing. It reminded him of how his mother and her people would speak. They were all gone now and he had been alone and lonely for too long. Saying I do would change that.

"I do," he said flinging back the sheet and launching out of bed. With a satisfied smile he began a mental list of everything he had to do before two o'clock when he was scheduled to meet Hope at her place.

Hours later, after Ted Pettigrew's call to the department

because someone had knifed all four of his car's tires—perhaps because his next Letters to the Editor column showed nothing close to "fair and balanced"—and after Ellis called complaining that a fifteen-thousand-dollar bull had been painted black and white like a skunk, Lyon made it to Hope's cozy haven. When he pulled into the third garage and saw that her Mercedes was there and the hardwood door was open for him, he felt an instant sense of homecoming.

"Hi, honey, I'm home," he called cheerfully hoping she'd heard none of the nonsense going around town and would be amused.

She emerged immediately from her room wearing a short, white satin robe with her hair up in a towel. "Are you all right?"

"Sure. I'm not late, am I?"

"Don't put on a front for me, Lyon. I heard about Pettigrew's tires and my father's bull."

"Since you didn't call me, I hoped you were buried in work and missed the commotion."

"The tire thing maybe…if Ted hadn't called my office and threatened that if he got one inkling of evidence that I was somehow behind that—"

"He did what?" Lyon interjected. "Why blame you?"

"The real reason? Because I joined Gus in protest and cancelled my ongoing ad in the paper, too. But you know Pettigrew, he would never come out and say that. He claims someone saw a lemon-yellow VW on the street where the paper's offices are located on the night of the alleged attack. Guess whose assistant drives a lemon-yellow VW?"

"Freddie." Fredericka Darlington was forty-something-year-old divorcée who wore drab clothes, sensible shoes, and seemed to never speak unless asked a direct question. The idea that Freddie would drive such a youthful, fun car, let alone be part of something so violent had Lyon shaking his head. "Did you ask her if she was involved?"

"Of course not. The post office is diagonally across the street. She goes there for me at least three times a day, often more. She has every right to be there." Hope pulled off the towel and fluffed her hair that she'd protected from the shower water. Then she blotted her face with the towel. "What I did do is ask for Ted's witness' name, which is supposed to be supplied upon request. Needless to say he demurred."

"Knowing how few friends he has, I'll bet he has his mother write the letters." But tired of Pettigrew interfering with their day, Lyon gave her a head-to-toe admiring look. "Interesting wedding dress...although I'm not sure I'm eager for anyone else to see it."

"Very funny. Bet I'm ready before you are," she said with all of the dignity her petite frame could muster.

She did beat him, too. When Lyon returned to the kitchen, she was already there and her lace-covered satin sheath made him stop in mid-step. "Stunning," he murmured.

"Thank you, but this bracelet has to come off," she said turning her back to him at the same time she tried to brush her hair to the side. "See this?"

"What?" he asked coming to her.

"My bracelet is hung on my dress."

"Hold still," he said carefully getting the fine threads freed from a bit of gold wire here and a hook there. When she was totally freed, he leaned closer and touched his lips to her nape. "Almost as good as new. There's just a tiny bit of threading pulled out of its weave."

"Thank you," she said again, this time more breathlessly.

She looked like she belonged on top of a cake and, yet, Lyon thought belatedly, they weren't even going to have a cake. She was being badly shortchanged on what should have been the happiest day of her life. Even those diamond and pearl earrings that matched the bracelet looked like serious heirlooms. They made him embarrassed for his simple band and he thought that he wasn't just marrying an heiress, he was marrying a goddess.

"Love the suit," she said taking in his newest purchase.

The gray silk had already been purchased for her wedding when he decided that he couldn't be the best man. He never got around to telling Will that and he saw no wisdom in explaining the particulars to Hope either. He simply said, "Glad you like it. If you're ready, we'd better get the rings and go."

He didn't want to hear his inner voice tell him to offer her a last chance to back out. Seeing her like this—radiant, her glossy hair almost as bright as her dark eyes, her perfect skin glowing—he had never wanted anyone more.

When they were westbound on the highway, Lyon noticed Hope fingering her small leather clutch purse a few times and smooth her skirt once too often. "Nervous?"

"No…well, maybe a little." She glanced toward him. "You?"

"Not a bit, unless you make a sudden grab for the doorknob."

She gasped and covered her tummy. "No worry about that. I'm just hoping you won't end up regretting this…or resenting me."

"Don't waste your time."

When they entered the outskirts of Sherman, Lyon pulled into a parking lot of a small strip mall and stopped in front of a flower shop. "Back in a minute."

"Oh, really?" Hope gave him a bemused smile. "What did you do?"

"Well, what's a wedding without flowers?"

He returned as quickly as promised carrying a bouquet of delicate, red tea roses framed by white lace.

Hope gasped, "How exquisite!" as she accepted the token. She lowered her face to the blossoms for several seconds. "Lyon, this is simply perfect."

He simply smiled, pleased that he had managed to make the occasion a little more special. She would have no family or friends. He hoped she understood that he knew what this was costing her.

At the courthouse, Lyon parked in the rear as Ed Viney directed and were met at the entryway by his secretary, who led them to his office. Grinning broadly, Ed shook Lyon's hand and kissed Hope's cheek. "My! I hope you two know how pleased I am to do this," he said.

His enthusiasm was contagious and Hope's smile deepened. "We appreciate you and your staff's time and discretion."

Ed was so committed to this little covert operation, he brought them into his office where his wife stood with his secretary to act as their witnesses. "I'll tell you how long I've know these two," he said as he introduced them. "My wife is Connie, and her sister is Bonnie, and I always get their names turned around, but Bonnie hasn't quit, and Connie hasn't filed for a divorce."

Lyon had discussed the ceremony with Ed and without explaining anything personal asked for the simplest service. So the older man had barely begun before he was saying, "Under the power vested me, I now pronounce you man and wife."

He could kiss his bride.

Looking down at her upturned face, calm, hopeful, so very lovely, Lyon framed her face with his hands and touched his lips to hers once, twice, and on the third time he kissed her wishing her to see his heart and offer him hers.

"Congratulations, Chief and Mrs. Teague."

The cheery greeting reluctantly brought him back to earth and they were instructed to sign the license, then Bonnie and Connie added their signatures.

"I so enjoyed this," said Ed's wife, Connie with merry eyes and a bubbly personality to match her every-which-way curls. "The way you two looked at each other and kissed was just like in one of my favorite romance novels." She brought out a camera from her legal-brief-size purse. "I see you didn't bring one to remember the day. Mind if I do that for you?"

"We completely forgot," Hope said, her cheeks still pink from Connie's effusive descriptions.

With Connie's direction, several poses were snapped. Lyon hoped the one with him standing behind Hope and his arms around her came out best; he wanted to set it on his desk in the office.

"It'll take a few weeks, but you'll receive the registered copy in the mail," Ed finally told them.

They didn't pass anyone on their way to the car and once inside, they were both silent. Lyon ached to reach for Hope and kiss her again, ask for her reassurance that she wasn't sorry, but all he managed was a gruff, "Too late now."

"Now it's time for the hard part," she amended.

Lyon frowned. "You weren't wanting to go straight over there and tell him, were you?"

"We should, but…would you mind if we waited until

tomorrow, or the day after? It seems so wrong to taint that ceremony."

"You won't hear any arguments from me." He would do whatever she asked to keep her looking as she was at her flowers and ring. It thrilled him to think that she was even fractionally as caught up in the moment as she appeared to be.

They talked and laughed all the way home. Hope asked for more stories about how he knew Ed, and Lyon teased her about how Ed's wife and sister-in-law tried to get her to throw her bouquet because Bonnie was presently single and wishing, but Hope couldn't make herself let go of it.

When they entered the house, they found another surprise—a one-layer cake with a bride and groom in the center. The frosting was cream cheese painstakingly spread, but the few crumbs around the plate suggested the cake was chocolate. What really had them chuckling was that Molly had used a black marking pen to try and color the bride's blond hair black.

"Now you know why I love her and Tan," Hope said.

"We should invite them over for some."

"They'd decline, but I'll call in a minute to thank them for us and promise to bring them each a piece in the morning." She gestured with her flowers. "Why don't you change and get the grill started? I'll see you in a few minutes."

While Lyon wished it was a real wedding day and that he could follow her to the master bedroom where they could help each other undress in the amber glow of the late afternoon sunlight, then make love until they knew each other by touch in the dark, he knew there were blessings to count with things as they were. At least she was bound to him now; all he had to do was build on his patience and her trust. He knew she considered him a friend, hopefully her dearest friend. Such friendships had been known to evolve into deeper love.

Only that wasn't enough.

There was great passion inside of Hope, and he wanted that, too. He'd seen it often enough to where it had fostered a gnawing hunger in him, saw it in those mysterious, exotic eyes, when she fought for others' rights, and spoke of protecting his job. How did he direct it at himself?

Show her.

The thought had him staring into space as in his school days when he faced a blank page when he was expected to write a term paper. English was his first language, but that didn't help the words move to paper. Adding to the challenge, he had always gotten along with women, but never had to woo one before. That wasn't arrogance; he simply had never had a relationship that interested him beyond that of mutual gratification. Like a lazy mind, an under-exercised heart was showing its disadvantages.

He knew one thing for certain—he didn't only want to seduce Hope, he wanted what his parents had found. Whatever happened, he decided, pulling at his tie, it mustn't be because he didn't try hard enough.

Chapter Four

"Are you sure about this?" Hope asked Lyon as he shut off the engine to his police car.

He'd picked her up ten minutes ago at the house for their ten o'clock meeting with her father, although Ellis didn't know the appointment was for both of them. Lyon had raised his eyebrows at the idea that a daughter was kept to such formal conditions, and she'd had to explain that there was no such thing as just dropping by. Ellis had made that clear when she refused to move back into the house after her mother's death. The protocol was fine with her, since it somewhat protected her from impromptu visits from him; however, she didn't doubt for a moment that he would show up at her front door if he was determined to see her. It was sad testimony to think that was the second, and not third or fourth, reason why she'd put in the electronic gate system.

"I told you," Lyon replied. "You handling this alone is not an option."

It wasn't that Hope wasn't grateful; she simply yearned for what they'd had yesterday—the peaceful atmosphere, the companionship as they'd cooked together and filled in the gaps of what life was like when each was away in school or jobs prior to their current work. It was hardly a conventional evening considering that they were supposed to be on their honeymoon, but knowing how her father was apt to react in a few moments made her yearn to turn back the clock for a few more hours alone with Lyon.

"I don't suppose you'd consider leaving your gun in the car?" she asked.

Lyon gave her a mild look. "Let's just get this over with."

Releasing their seat belts, they exited the car and walked together up the four stairs to the veranda of the two-story federal-style mansion that had been built less than two decades after the Alamo. The house was recognized by the state historical society and had been on the Cedar Grove tour of homes three times that Hope could remember. Two large concrete urns framed the front door bearing junipers trimmed into spiral topiaries. The structure could be a courthouse the way it looked now—well-tended, but extremely spare in adornment, and aloof, like the owner.

The front door opened before Hope could ring the bell. A slender man in a black suit and red-and-black striped tie about the same age and coloring as her father nodded his head in a nominal bow and stepped aside to let them enter.

"Miss Harrell, Chief Teague."

"Hello, Greenleaf," Hope replied to her father's longtime butler. "It's nice to see you."

"You as well, miss. You'll find him in the study."

That was as friendly as her father's employee was apt to dare get and she wasn't about to make things more difficult for him except for one question. "Is Mrs. Crandall okay? I haven't seen her in town in a while."

"She broke a toe almost two weeks ago, Miss. I'm doing the shopping and errands that I can until she can wear regular shoes again."

"I'm so sorry. I had no idea." Needless to say, her father hadn't shared that bit of news. "Please tell her that I asked about her and send my sympathies," she said. "And let me know if there is anything I can do for either of you."

"I will. Thank you, Miss Hope."

Greenleaf didn't invite warm fuzzies and using her first name was the only sign that he recognized her sincerity and concern, but Hope could never fault his service or discipline, and she felt much the same about Mrs. Crandall, although she barely knew her. Hope had moved out when their long-time housekeeper Naomi Jobs retired and Mrs. C had joined the staff.

As the butler stood back to let them cross the expansive foyer, Hope didn't attempt to explain or reminisce about the decor with Lyon, even though this was his first time there; however, she did pause so Lyon could get a closer look at the full-size portrait of her mother on her wedding day on the wall beside the study doors.

"She was beautiful," he murmured. "Except for the more formal gown, that could be a portrait of you."

Despite her awareness that Greenleaf was watching, Hope touched his arm. "You always say the right thing."

"Your hand is cold," he noted, covering it with his. He squeezed gently, his look reassuring.

Hope started to reply when the double doors swung open. She pivoted neatly, her hair and flower-print skirt flaring. Adjusting her red leather purse strap on the shoulder of a short white jacket, she settled her expression into a polite smile.

"Hello, Dad. How are you?"

"What's he doing here?" Ellis demanded, his gaze immediately narrowing on Lyon.

Hope suspected he'd seen them drive up and walk up to the front door, since the floor to ceiling windows in the study faced the circular driveway. But since he hated being caught unawares and she had refused to tell him what this meeting was about, he was at a disadvantage. A price was in the process of being exacted.

"We came to share a few things with you."

Not quite as tall as Lyon, or as toned, he remained an impressive physical specimen for a man turning sixty-two by Christmas. Even his lush head of hair still had some blonde in it. His tan sports jacket over crisp white shirt and pressed jeans might exude a casual first glance, but upon closer examination, they were undoubtedly tailored for him, and his black boots were sharkskin, not cowhide.

"You know perfectly well you made me believe my appointment was with you and you alone," Ellis replied, his baritone voice rough from shouting too many orders in corrals and meeting rooms than from scotch and cigars. "And you have ten minutes before I have to leave."

"Heading to the hospital?"

"What the devil for?" he asked, doing a 180-degree turn and retreating back into his office. His demeanor was such that he was giving notice that he didn't care if they followed or not.

"To purge whatever is making you sound like a stopped-up septic tank."

He spun around and looked like he was about to grind her into his lunch, but abruptly burst into a single bark of laughter. "Whatever it is you want," he said pointing at her, "that crack just cost you ten percent more than it would have."

"Then lucky for us that we're not here to negotiate," Hope replied. "How was your dinner party?"

"Fine, no thanks to you. Summer Isadore graciously agreed to take your place."

Summer was a dozen years her senior and so hardly what Jack Nolan might be in the market for, but always receptive to an invitation from Ellis, so Hope doubted there was no hardship involved. She owned *Summer's Ladies,* a boutique for women like her—affluent, discerning, and always on the prowl for greener pastures. As much as Hope tried to shop locally to support entrepreneurs, she wouldn't be crossing that threshold, unless she saw smoke billowing in the display window and had forgotten how to dial 911.

When Hope failed to take the bait, Ellis offered a cranky, "All right, so you won this round. I'll admit to being curious. What's up?"

"Lyon and I simply wanted to inform you before we make a formal announcement. We're married."

He looked from one of them to the other. "The hell you say."

Hope held out her left hand so he could see the ring. "And before you say something you're going to regret, you'd better know that I'm going to have a baby."

"His?"

"Careful," Lyon warned him.

Ellis turned away from them, his hands fisted at his side. "How dare you?" he finally rasped.

It was impossible to tell if that was meant for her or Lyon, but as far as Hope was concerned it was the same thing. "If you're accusing either one of us of something," she began, "please remember that we're both well over the age of consent and we hardly need the blessing of Vatican *West*. But if you're singling me out, consider that I could say the same thing to you for making a private loan to Will behind my back."

That startled her father and his about face wasn't smooth. "He told you?"

"Right after I broke our engagement."

A muscle under her father's right eye twitched. "Why did you do a fool thing like that?"

"Why is my not so subtle accusation so easy for you to dismiss?" Hope shook her head. "Mother would never have dreamed to give you cause to doubt her."

"Apples and oranges. Your mother was barely twenty when I married her. Will was a man, not a boy."

"You aren't going to claim age gives you the right to lie as well as cheat? Poor Mother," she said almost to herself. "She had it rougher than I even guessed."

Ellis circled his massive oak desk and sat down heavily in a burgundy leather chair. "That's not fair."

"Inconvenient truths, Father."

For several seconds Ellis looked out the nearest window, his jaw squared and his gray eyes hard. Hope once thought him as handsome as Robert Redford; however, while still in braids, she'd grasped that he had none of the actor-turned-director-turned renaissance man's finessed quali-ties. He remained handsome in his element, much the way a free predator could be artistically and scientifically mesmerizing, yet dangerous in the wild. Hope harbored a healthy wariness of that man.

When Ellis fixed Lyon with his gaze, he demanded, "And what do you have to say for yourself?"

"To you, nothing. But you might give your daughter your blessing."

"I'll take the H-brand to your cunning hide first."

"That would be fair if I thought you were concerned for her and her alone. But exactly how long do you think keeping your foot on her neck will work for you?"

"Why you—"

As Ellis pushed himself out of his chair, Hope stepped into his line of vision. "Lyon is the least manipulative man you'll ever meet. The least like you. Is that why Will had your full support? He was more of a son to you, a chip off the old block, than I'm a daughter?"

"You must be pregnant," Ellis spat. "You're getting emotional."

Lyon took careful hold of Hope's elbow. "We're done here, let's go."

Hope stood her ground. "This was a courtesy visit, but hear this—meddle in my private life or continue to support any of that nonsense going on in town to remove Lyon, and be assured—Clyde and Mercy aren't the only people who will know how Will was sweating to hide his business mistakes." Part of that was an educated guess, but it proved fruitful.

The arrogance of power was draining from her father's face. "You'd ruin the reputation of the man you were supposed to marry?"

"He was doing just fine on his own. But what is despicable is that you were willing to see me locked in a marriage that would break my heart. That I won't forget or easily forgive."

She let Lyon direct her out of the room and the house, grateful that there was no further sign of Greenleaf, although she suspected he wasn't far away. As for her and Lyon, they didn't speak again until they were in the car and almost at the end of the driveway.

"Remind me never to push you into a corner," Lyon said as though reciting the time and temperature.

Closing her eyes wasn't enough. Moaning, Hope covered her face with her hands. "He's right. I got emotional when I meant to stay so calm and focused. "

"You were terrific."

"You have to say that, you're stuck with me."

"No," he drawled. "I don't. A wedding vow doesn't mean unconditional support, especially for a bad idea—though I'm not saying this was. But it does mean recognizing what this meeting cost you. I admire your strength. You've lived under that roof for almost two decades and have seen the bodies of his enemies and victims pile up in bankruptcy court and cemeteries. I admit that once upon a time, I thought you were a bit of a Girl Scout. I'd already changed my mind since then, but my respect for you grew the width and depth of another ocean today."

Hope didn't want the compliment to matter so much, but she was feeling ultra exposed having said so much in front of him. "Girl Scout, huh? I guess a hug is a hug."

"I can do better."

They were well out of sight of the estate and Lyon turned into a wooded driveway where he shifted into Park and released his seat belt. Then he slid back the seat and released Hope's buckle and deftly lifted her onto his lap.

"Lyon…" she gasped. She found herself eye to eye with him. "This is crazy."

"Humor me," he replied. "It's either this or I take you to the ER to make sure your blood pressure isn't about to rupture a vein or hurt the baby."

With that he leaned her back over his arm and claimed her mouth with his, kissing her the way he'd been wanting for too long to remember. She was immediately responsive and pliant in his arms, her lips parting to his probing, her back arching as he coaxed her closer, as close as he could get her. She smelled like heaven, she felt like a dream, and her taste went to his head faster than any drink could. Craving much more, Lyon withdrew his tongue and slid his lips across her cheek to press against the side of her neck.

"Now you may need to get me to the hospital," she told him.

He was immediately contrite. "Did I hurt you lifting you over this confounded clutter?"

He was referring to the console where there was everything from more gadgets to communication gear. "No more than a bump or two. I was talking about that kiss."

"I'm breaking my own rule to not take advantage."

"You aren't. But you did say this arrangement could be anything I wanted it to be. I liked the kiss, Lyon. I liked it a lot."

His chest rose and fell as he breathed deeply, and he brushed his thumb against her lower lip. "I hope you mean that because I need to do it again."

Their second kiss had her wrapping her arms around his neck. That crushed her breasts against his hard chest, and she could feel their hearts leap and pound anew as his tongue coaxed hers to kiss him back in that steamy, languid way, as if they had all the time in the world. Hope felt her body heat as though the air conditioner wasn't running and it was triple-digit August instead of the middle of May. He made her wish they were home instead of here and that he would do more than run his hands up and down her back and torment her with only brushing the backs of his fingers over the outermost swell of her breast. She yearned to feel his skin touching hers, and his breath—

"I have to answer that," Lyon said sighing.

"Answer what?"

He grinned and his chest shook slightly from laughter. "Dispatch wants a check in."

That was when she heard a discreet clicking. Realizing it was a mic check, she tried to return to her seat, but he stayed her and just searched beneath the hem of her skirt to find the handheld device.

"Go ahead, Buddy. Over."

"Chief, Mr. Pettigrew is here."

Lyon exchanged looks with Hope, then he checked his dashboard clock. "I'm about twenty minutes out. Tell him I can call him later if he can't wait."

"Hang on. Over."

While Buddy conferred with the editor of Cedar Grove's newspaper, Lyon helped Hope back into her seat. His caresses left her ultra-sensitive to his touch and her subtle shiver and squirming to get her seat belt fastened must have telegraphed something to him.

"Are you okay?"

"Sure."

"That guy has the worst timing on the planet."

He sounded regretful, his voice as tender as his touch, but

she was thinking of how far she would have been willing to go. In who knows whose driveway? In broad daylight!

"I need to get to my office anyway." She smoothed her hair while he took the call back, and willed her heart to stop pounding like some over-wound toy.

Pettigrew would wait. Lyon said, "All right, see you eleven at the latest."

"Doesn't sound good," she said after he disconnected and replaced the mic. "Do you suppose my father called him the moment we left?"

"Not enough time for him to conjure a plan and order Ted to the station. This is something else. Please tell me you're okay?"

She gave him a bright look. "Fine."

"No, you're not." He placed his hand on her cheek to keep her face toward his. "What is it? Did I go too fast?"

"We're not preteens experimenting on a first date," she replied, her sardonic tone for herself, not him. So why did she suddenly feel so unlike herself, and wrong?

"No, thank heaven we're not." His focus was wholly on her lips. "I'll be hard pressed to listen to Ted let alone anyone else the rest of the day. All I'll be thinking about is you."

The push and pull of emotions continued to war within her until she groaned. "My father was right," she said with chagrin. "I'm all hormones."

"Forget about your father. He doesn't have a—" Lyon swore under his breath. "We can't have this conversation right now." He shifted roughly into reverse and backed out of the dirt driveway.

Hope grimaced at his rough handling of the car. She didn't blame him for being frustrated with her. She wasn't all that happy with herself, either.

"Do you *have* to go into the office?" he asked about a mile down the road. "It might do you good to take the day off."

"I can't. I have to prepare for a meeting right after lunch. It's a new client."

"Then at least promise me you'll call your doctor? The OBGYN you mentioned."

"I did before you picked me up. But Dr. Winslow can't see me until this time next week." She sent him an apologetic look. "I'm okay, Lyon. I'm sorry that I worried you."

But when he dropped her off at the house and he leaned over to kiss her goodbye, she turned her head in the last second and the kiss barely skimmed her cheek.

"See you later," she said and quickly jumped from the squad car. Seeing he was about to say her name or say something, she slammed shut the door and dashed to get her own vehicle.

Lyon turned the air conditioner on high for the trip back to town. If he had a cup with ice left over from a cold drink, he would have tossed that into his lap. Let Pettigrew and the whole office think what they would when he walked in dripping wet.

He ached and he worried and neither sensation was pleasant. Why had Hope gone—not cool, but distant and antsy on him? That wasn't hormones, or not all hormones. Had she been telling the truth that she was okay? She wouldn't have responded like she did if she wasn't.

Patience, he reminded himself. Married a day and already he had to remind himself about that oath. It was the delicacy of her clothes that had almost driven him crazy. Her blouse was as thin as a scarf, her bra as fine as her lace mantilla. Her nipples had been taut for him. When her jacket had parted, he'd seen that clearly. Whatever had made her not want to give him a real goodbye kiss, she wanted him as much as he wanted her. He had to take comfort in that.

Ted Pettigrew did not enjoy being kept waiting. When Lyon entered the station, he launched at him like a giraffe protecting a watering hole—narrow head and skinny neck first and lanky arms and legs playing catch up.

"There are allegations that you're using a city vehicle for personal use," he declared.

He was oblivious of Buddy, who gave him a pained look, since Pettigrew's voice was like a boom box and Buddy was trying to hear a radio call from one of the other officers in the field. Cooper Jones even leaned out of his office, and it took something considerable to tear him away from a forensics report.

One thing Lyon knew he was guilty of nothing—except to driving home and back to the station. "If this is a fishing expedition, you're wasting your time," he replied snatching up the pink phone message slips Buddy held up for him, and continuing to his office.

"It's been recorded that on the 5th, 7th, then the 10th through yesterday, either you didn't return to your apartment until late, or you didn't return at all." Pettigrew looked over his frameless lenses at him. "Can you prove these records are incorrect?"

Once behind his desk, Lyon glanced up at him. "Records? You mean notes, don't you, Ted? Or are you wasting the paper's money on a private detective?"

Only mildly set back by Lyon correcting him, Ted waved his pad dismissively. "It's been a hectic morning and

I misspoke. This is a personal log and, no, I won't share my sources."

"What did you do, plant your mother-in-law with a bag of cheddar popcorn in the parking lot of my apartment?" Once in a while, when all of the Letters to the Editor were critical of Ted's editorials, he would have his mother-in-law write something on his behalf. Who knew what else he'd asked of the poor woman?

"You'd be wise to take this seriously—and appreciate my attempt to give you an opportunity to defend yourself."

"I always take you seriously, Ted. That's why I'm telling you once and with complete frankness that my vehicle was not in use after hours on those dates."

"You haven't even checked your calendar or log."

"Don't have to. Those are memorable dates to me." He sat down and shot the disgruntled newspaperman a benign look. "Is there anything else?"

"You don't seem to grasp the importance of this—I'm going to be running an editorial on the critics who feel your job performance has left a bad taste in some people's mouths," Pettigrew replied.

An editorial, not a news article. "That's your prerogative, although I will say that I'm deeply disappointed."

"And I can quote you as not interested in helping yourself?"

Lyon pointed to the top envelope on his desk. "The autopsy report on Will Nichols came in this morning." He hadn't told Hope because he hadn't wanted to add to any nerves she was feeling before meeting with Ellis. "The medical examiner said that Will broke his neck during the rollovers. If he'd only had a partial break when I reached him and had I succeeded in pulling him out, I might have been guilty of involuntary manslaughter. As it is, all you have is the complaint by a woman who was messing around with an engaged man. You go with that and you're going to look pretty ridiculous. Anything else is criticism by people who don't care for me or for not signing on to their politics. That's not a firing offense."

"Can the press have a copy of that report?"

"Not before I share the results with his next of kin."

"What was his alcohol reading?"

Lyon winced inwardly, but enunciated slowly, "After I tell the family, Ted."

As soon as Pettigrew strode out of his office, Lyon dialed Hope's number. He didn't want to make this call—not after they'd parted so unsatisfactorily, but he was afraid Ted would call her wanting a statement. He couldn't not warn her.

"Harrell Consultants," a scratchy voice began. "May I help you?"

"Freddie, this is Chief Teague. Is Ms. Harrell available?"

"Oh! Yes, sir, she just walked in. Hold please."

It took Hope a good while before she picked up—long enough to make Lyon wonder if she was trying to avoid taking the call. Finally he heard a click and her soft voice. "Yes?"

"Sorry to bother you when you've only just arrived. Do you have anyone in your office?"

"No, why?"

"I wanted to beat Ted Pettigrew. I was afraid he would get hold of you before I could."

"Oh, God, what's happened?"

"Nothing you didn't know or suspect, but you'd still have been caught off guard. The autopsy report came in.

Actually, it was here early this morning, but I didn't think the time was right to tell you."

"I see."

Did she? Lyon prayed so. "Hope, his neck was broken on impact." A barely audible sound came over the line and his heart twisted. "Damn, I'm sorry for telling you like this. Are you okay?"

"Yes. You're right, I was prepared for that, but it still delivers a kick."

"It does. Pettigrew wanted to know his alcohol level. I told him that I wasn't releasing any other results until I reported to the next of kin. I'll call Clyde next."

"Yes, thank you. I wouldn't want to be the one."

"No, of course not." Lyon stared at the report. "He was well over the limit for alcohol, Hope. More so than I would have guessed, which means he'd been indulging elsewhere."

Hope drew in a ragged breath. "I can't listen to any more, Lyon. I—I have to get out of here."

"I'll be right there."

"No, you have work to—"

The phone went dead. Lyon's heart plunged, but he didn't give himself time to wonder if she'd done it on purpose or if she couldn't help it because she was about to be sick. He was out of his office and heading for the front door even as he gave directives to Buddy. "I'm out for anything but an emergency," he told him. "You can reach me by the radio."

"Do you need backup? Anything?"

"No. Tell Cooper the Nichols autopsy is on my desk—for his eyes only. If anyone else calls about it, delay them."

Lyon made it back to the house just as the first garage door was closing. He triggered the third one to open and saw Hope already at the storm door fumbling with keys. When she saw him, she covered her face with the tissues crumpled in her hand and turned away.

Lyon barely stopped the car before he was rushing to her. "Are you sick? Do you need the bathroom first?"

"No, I've already been there, done that. Now I'm just mortified."

"Don't be. You've been heading for this from the beginning and operating on sheer willpower. It's a wonder you've held it together as long as you did." His arm around her for support, he unlocked the door and helped her inside. Feeling how unsteady she was, once they were through to the kitchen, he took her purse and set it on the bar, then swept her into his arms and carried her to her bedroom.

She moaned and hid her face against his shoulder. "Please don't do this."

"Hush. It's going to be all right."

This was his first time coming to this side of the house. He barely noticed the pretty Santa Fe colors and elegant cherry furnishings, but the bright sunshine that was making the bedroom migraine bright immediately drew his concern. As soon as he laid her on the turquoise and green bedspread, he went to the windows and cranked the mini-blinds closed. That turned the room into a dusky oasis.

Returning to the bed, he saw that Hope had immediately folded into a tight fetal position. "Let's get you more comfortable," he said easing her up. He slipped off her red strappy heels and placed them on the far side of the night stand, then started on her jacket. "That's it," he said soothingly as she strived to help him. "Take your time. Should I call Molly?"

"No! She'd only get upset. I'll be fine as soon as I rest for a few minutes."

Lyon doubted it since she couldn't say that much without her voice cracking. He couldn't stand it. Settling onto the edge of the bed, he began coaxing her into his arms until he was cradling her. He thought things were going well…and then she burst into tears.

Lyon hated the ragged sounds that ripped through her. He couldn't imagine what she was feeling, caught in a world where she knew a fiancé hadn't loved her enough, a father she couldn't trust, and a mother long gone and unable for her to console or confide in. His words would be wholly inadequate right now. All he could do was rock her and hope that regretting their marriage wasn't part of her toppling world.

"You'll think this horrible," she said fighting for control, "but all I keep thinking is that…he could have killed both of us. All of us."

Lyon couldn't let his mind go there, and yet *she* had to. Her heart was shuddering in aftershocks for the tiny life she carried inside her, her body turning cold from the grim shadows that carried the echo, "What if?" She was right— as soon as he'd known her condition, Will should have driven like he had the world's most precious cargo in that truck. Better yet, Will should have pulled over and waited for him to get Hope home. The problem was Will couldn't deal with anyone coming before him. That character flaw would have ended his professional career if the injury hadn't, and it would have eventually killed Hope's love for him once she saw that even a baby came second to his own voracious ego. Hope was also right that Will Nichols would have been a perfect son-in-law for Ellis. Second to losing her mother, this was probably the worst day in her life.

"You have to take care now, too, sweetheart," he said

gently stroking her hair. "Making yourself sick can hurt the baby, as easily as anything else."

"You're right." She took a deep, sustaining breath. "I guess I just felt betrayed all over again, and then so angry. With myself, too."

Smiling to himself, Lyon kissed her hair. "Good idea. After all, you're the only one who was meant to have perfect judgment and never make a mistake."

That won a muffled laugh from her. "It's about time you noticed that."

Having stepped away from being trapped in that bad psychological place, she was sounding stronger. It was time to win another concession from her. "Are you going to reschedule that appointment you mentioned?"

"It wouldn't be fair to the poor woman not to. In fact, I may have Freddie close early and have her come over to tell her what's going on."

More good news, Lyon thought. "She's your right hand. She needs to know you're with child." That would also allow him to check on Hope without her knowing it.

"Freddie's a bit offbeat and hard to figure out, but even she will take this better knowing first that I'm married. I'll try to hold off the pregnancy news until next month."

That might be a good idea even if she didn't try to let it be perceived that he was the father. They were going to hear plenty of criticism as it was from the elopement announcement. "Then I'll start letting it be known at the office, too. Buddy looked like a grouper with his big eyes and working mouth when I left." He told her that he'd just stated he needed to go and to only radio if there was an emergency.

"You do need to get back, but I want you to know I appreciate this."

He stroked her back. "Just as long as you aren't upset with me—I mean about earlier."

Disengaging herself, Hope sat up and dabbed at the moisture still clinging to her lashes. It was a good sign if she was starting to worry about makeup damage, but not so good that she could only meet his eyes for a second before glancing away.

"I didn't mean to come off as a tease, Lyon."

"How do you figure you did?"

"I realized my, um, behavior had left you…uncomfortable."

"Aroused."

"It's only been a week since the funeral!"

He knew exactly what she was driving at—the same thing anyone who had faced life and death could have experienced. "What you're going through is natural," he told her. "Although I'd like to think that I had something to do with things."

"Of course you did," she said. "That's what made it worse."

"Worse?"

"More difficult to come to terms with. I value your opinion of me, Lyon. I didn't want you to think that despite feeling what I did, that I would have…you know."

"Let down your guard with anyone else?" If he wasn't so concerned that she quit beating herself up, he could have laughed at her cute way of trying to talk about sex without using the terminology. He folded her closer and laid his cheek on top of her head. "I knew that. But it's nice to hear anyway."

"That's good because I couldn't bear it if you—"

"I'm here for you. I know you're going to be going through changes and there'll be…"

"Struggles."

"I was going to say sexual tension, but wild woman that you are, I was concerned about triggering your libido and having to stop you from stripping off your clothes."

Hope gasped and pushed away from him, only to see his mischievous grin. "You are horrible," she said, although she couldn't repress a smile herself.

And she was beautiful even with a shiny, red nose and the hint of raccoon eyes. "Hope, promise me you won't keep me having to play twenty guesses? If you need to be held, I'll hold you. Taking a cold shower later is much easier than working up an ulcer because I don't know what's made you shut me out."

Her expression softened and she laid her hand against his cheek. "What did I do to deserve you?"

"Don't be too flattering, I do have my limits. Don't ask me to watch when you get around to craving pickles and ice cream."

"Yuck. That doesn't sound remotely appealing. Thank you," she added quietly. After she noticed his gaze lowering to her mouth, she leaned close and touched her lips to his.

"Again, please," he said keeping his eyes closed.

She did as he asked, this time lingering and gently brushing her lips back and forth against his. He liked the way their noses caressed, too, and wisps of her hair acted like fingertips stroking his face.

"Better." He had to swallow because even these sweet caresses were starting to raise his temperature and leave him parched. "I am, after all, the man who is going to endure watching you turn green from morning sickness and be asked for back rubs when you get geometrically imbalanced."

"Not necessarily, smarty. I've had a standing appointment for a few years with a massage therapist in town," she said against his lips. "Like the yoga, it's preventative care."

Before she could withdraw, he gave into the need to part her lips further and kissed her in a manner that caressed her the way he ached to explore the rest of her body. Her soft sounds of appreciation and yearning soon tempted him to lean her back against the bedspread and stretch out beside her.

"You're clicking, Chief."

Lyon realized he was being summoned. Buddy was giving his discreet indication requesting a check-in before he was forced to make a verbal request. With a sigh, Lyon pushed himself to his feet.

"Guess you know where I'm headed," he told Hope.

"Will you be home for dinner? I'm thinking of calling over Molly after all. We could make something nice."

She really needed to rest, but if some quiet time with sweet-natured Molly did the trick, that was good, too. "Short of a Caribbean cruise liner missing its dock and carving its way all the way up here, you bet," he replied.

"See you then."

Chapter Five

Hope didn't get morning sickness. What she did was develop an extreme taste for all foods with a Southwestern flavor and had to consciously work at not indulging three times a day. By the Fourth of July she had worked through her Rolodex of her mother's personal recipes, and the three other specialized cookbooks she owned. She was eyeing a recipe online when Molly entered the kitchen with a basket of roses from the front yard.

"How does grilled snapper stuffed with jalapeños sound?" she asked her. "My mouth is already watering."

Molly hugged the colorful blooms to her thin chest. "Jalapeños make my hands burn," she enunciated with care. Her expression reflected more than a little trepidation. "We can ask Tan to pick them. There are lots in the garden and they need to be picked, but he's been busy with the horses."

"Oh, sweetie, I can go pick them. I was just wondering

if it was just me and my crazy taste buds that thought the recipe sounded yummy."

She and Lyon were going to a town-and-church picnic in the city park and attendees were encouraged to donate to the buffet that would be open to the entire town. Lyon didn't want to go—he was already at the town's Liberty Parade and would be working tonight at the fireworks show. But while some people had taken their marriage announcement in stride—a few even relieved at what they saw as a better match—others had grown more negative than ever. Then, too, a client's freezer had gone out on them and they had several large red snappers that needed to be used up quickly.

"Let me put the roses in water," Molly said placing the basket on the counter beside the sink. "Then I'll go out with you and hold the hoe."

Bemused, Hope gave her a curious glance. "What for?"

"Tan saw a spread adder go in the garden yesterday. I'll watch and chase it away if it tries to come after you."

"I'm not afraid of a bluffing snake," Hope said with a laugh. But the thought of those critters meandering in her thriving garden did give her some pause. "You're sure he thought it was a non-venomous snake?"

"Oh, yes. He brought out his book and he showed me a picture. I hope it's gone. It looked like a cobra to me." Molly's expression grew vague and whimsical. "Tan is very smart. He reads all the time."

"And he's a good husband and groundskeeper. He wouldn't let a bad snake stay around here knowing you or I were going to be out there," Hope assured her. She squeezed the young woman's thin shoulder to bring her back from her mental wandering. If she didn't, sometimes

Molly could stay "gone" for minutes on end. "Okay, you see to the flowers and if you don't mind, wash the fish again that are soaking in the two big bowls in the refrigerator. I'll handle the pepper harvesting."

"Then I put the fish back in the refrigerator, right?"

"No, leave them soaking in the sink. We'll start the rest of the preparations as soon as I come back inside." The simplest tasks were sometimes a problem for Molly, but no one was more thorough and dependable when she got routines memorized.

Once outside, she saw Tan cleaning the hooves of Desiree, her gray pregnant mare. She let herself into the barn through a wooden gate and exited on the south side where he was bent over his task. "Good morning," she said. "I appreciate you getting that done today, Tan. But I hope you'll take it easy the rest of the day. It's a holiday."

Tan grinned at her, his eyes becoming little more than slits in his bronzed face. "Miss D follow me around all yesterday and paw ground. No more delay."

"I think she's training you as well as you're training her. Molly told me that you saw a spread adder in the garden. I just wanted you to know that if I yell, 'snake,' it's one of the more venomous varieties."

The slender, middle-aged man, who was her own height, shook his head. "No snake. I know you be coming out, so I look good. Find two fat tomato worm. Good fish bait. Molly and I catch dinner for later."

Luckily his wife loved fish. "Thank you, Tan. You spoil me. Are you and Molly going to come watch the fireworks tonight?"

He shook his head, then pointed. "Drive truck to middle of pasture and make picnic on back. Best view."

"How romantic. I'll envy you the privacy. I'm going to keep the chief company, since he wants to help his people monitor things. See you later."

She picked about a quart of peppers and returned to the kitchen where Molly was humming to herself and twisting a dish towel almost into a knot. Hope set her basket on the center workstation and peeled off her gloves.

"What's the problem, Molly?"

"I did wrong. I should let the machine answer the phone, but I wanted to help. You're busy and I was finished with the flowers and giving the fish a bath."

Oh, no, Hope thought. "Did the caller confuse you?"

"I asked the lady to not speak so fast. She got mad and called me the name."

Not *a* name, but *the* name. Hope immediately eased the towel from her hands and gave her a hug. She knew exactly what word the caller had used—*idiot*. Molly had heard it a great deal from her previous boyfriend even before the accident. Doctors had concluded it was the one thing she retained from that episode, although she had no memory of the man.

"I'm sorry, Molly, dear. That was rude of her. Can you remember who the caller was?"

"An M like me." Having no towel to twist, she began rubbing her wedding band like a worry stone. "I can't remember because it's not a real name. It's just a word."

Hope was getting as good as Tan at grasping what the young woman meant. She asked, "Was it Mercy?"

"That's the word!"

Why on earth had Mercy called here? Their last meeting in town, days after Hope and Lyon had made it public that they were married, had been stilted at best. Mercy acted as though she'd committed an offense against the entire Nichols family tree. Hope had clung to civility and lessons learned at her mother's skirt hem not to remind Mercy that until weeks ago, she had been the wife of a man who did little more than make excuses for why he couldn't find and keep gainful employment. While she'd taken in sewing and cleaned other people's houses, the senior-most Nichols strolled from store to coffee shop opining as to all that was wrong with this country. Only last year had Will succeeded in getting his deadbeat uncle a job with the city, but all that Clyde was qualified to do was burn gas driving around in a city truck. When the city was really shorthanded, he was the one holding the Slow sign at road repair locations. He couldn't even handle a Stop sign without causing a traffic jam. Most offensive was hearing through the grapevine that Clyde suspected the delay in getting the autopsy report on Will had been because Lyon was coercing the medical examiner to "doctor" the report in order to get attention off of himself. Hope fervently wished the Nichols to forget that they were once almost in-laws. What happened that Mercy should deign to phone here?

"Why don't you bring Tan something cool to drink?" she suggested to Molly. "He's almost finished making Desiree comfortable and even though it's still early, that sun has been baking him."

"He likes the lemonade you taught me to make. Can I take him some?"

"That's a great idea."

As soon as Molly shut the back door, carefully taking her husband the icy glass of lemonade, Hope hurried to her office and looked up the Nichols' number in the county phone book. Then she dialed it on the wireless phone. It rang twice before she received a recording that the number was no longer in service. The new number was the ranch one, which she dialed from her phone's directory, mentally reminding herself to remove it as soon as she finished with the call.

As she waited for the ringing to start, she thought how it hadn't taken the Nichols long at all to move in.

"Nichols residence."

"This is Hope," she said to Mercy. "I understand you called."

"How nice of you to call back so promptly," Mercy replied, her voice polite, but holding an unmistakable superior tone. "I wasn't sure you would get my message."

The woman was starting to get on her nerves. "You've probably forgotten my telling you about my helper Molly," Hope began, determined to keep her voice normal. "She was badly injured trying to escape a bad relationship. She had a difficult recovery and required much rehabilitation, but she is certainly capable of taking messages when given the chance."

After an awkward silence, Mercy said, "Now that you mention it, I do remember. I've had a great deal on my mind."

Disappointed that she wouldn't take ownership of her poor conduct, Hope replied, "Then don't let me keep you. What was it that you needed?"

"Well, as you can imagine, it's been nonstop stressful here since we probated William's estate. Since William was a bachelor and the place hadn't been given a proper cleaning in who knows how long, you can imagine the condition of the house."

Hope lifted her gaze to the ceiling and reached for more patience. Will had three sisters—one being the wife of one of his ranch hands—come by every week to clean and polish a different area of the house. In contrast, his uncle and aunt had lived in the same one-bedroom cottage in the oldest part of town since their marriage. And while the place was kept neat enough compared to some, during heavy rains a river flowed under the house that had no foundation and was precariously balanced on blocks. Hope remembered Will laughingly report that the floors were tilting more with each season and that one day the refrigerator was likely to end up on the back porch with the washing machine and probably finish turning that structure into a soggy pile of splinters and drowned termites.

"I don't know the name of the people who cleaned there regularly, Mercy," Hope told her. "I do know they were related to someone else who worked there. Ask Will's foreman. He'll know, but if you need me to refer someone, I can."

"First I need to inventory things properly. I can't allow strangers in here. But will your people have references that I can check out? I will require references."

Oh, my, Hope thought, she was certainly taking the Lady of the Manor role seriously. In fact, she suspected Mercy had known about the girls all along and had fired them the instant they came to the front door.

"I'm not sure," Hope replied. "You'll just have to ask them when the time comes. Is there anything else?"

"Since I have you on the phone, there is one small matter I wanted to clear up with you. Now that we have the court matters behind us, Clyde insists I get the Nichols family jewels."

Hope pressed her fingers to her lips. Did Mercy have any idea how the underlying excitement in her voice exposed her barely containable pleasure at the changes in their small lives?

"That sounds entirely legal and justified to me," she replied.

"You do? Well, thank you, Hope. Do you also understand that means if there's anything else found—I mean at the accident site or in the totaled truck at the salvage yard—it's to be returned here?"

What was obvious to Hope was that this entire conversation had been all a ploy to get to this subject. "Mercy, the authorities had my directives from the beginning for that to be the case, and if by chance someone forgot, I would have it redirected to you. Now I really must go and check on my oven. Take care and enjoy."

After disconnecting, she found herself feeling sorry for the woman. Her rudeness to Molly would not be forgotten, but Mercy undoubtedly thought money and property would open doors to a better society for her. She was about to find out it was far more complicated than that.

Once Molly returned smiling and happy again, she and Hope got the snappers stuffed and in the oven. They were just washing up when they heard the sound of the garage door opening. Lyon was home.

"Something smells mighty good," he said entering the kitchen.

As always when their gazes locked, Hope felt the world had righted itself somehow and a sense of peace and well-being seeped into her body. He looked hot and a bit tired, but his dark eyes sparkled as he gave her a discreet wink.

"Hot fish!" Molly declared wide-eyed for their achievement. "Not just hot from the oven. Hope picked every pepper in the garden—and all by herself. She cut them up, too, and never had to wash her hands once until the end. I couldn't do that."

Hope watched Lyon listen attentively and offer a comical grimace. "Me, either. I'd make a mistake and touch my eyes and the next thing I'd have my head under a faucet trying to cool off."

"Me, too," Molly echoed.

She looked pleased that she had something in common with a man who, until recently, she would never dare make eye contact with. Molly had believed the chief of police was way too important to speak to someone like her and Hope's own incomparable position in her world had risen to headier altitudes when she told Molly that she and Lyon were marrying.

"How was the parade?" Hope asked as he came up beside her and slipped his hand under her ponytail to caress her nape. That nominal touch sent a warm stream of pleasure down her spine.

"We had a stroller-motorcycle incident, but not much else."

"Goodness! I'd say that's enough. Was anyone hurt?"

"The bike. The stroller was empty except for a tote bag and canvas cooler full of baby bottles and water. The weight of that provided enough momentum to roll the buggy down a driveway ramp fast enough to knock over the bike and break a taillight. Otherwise, everyone seemed to enjoy themselves."

"That's a relief. You look ready for something cold to drink," Hope said.

"I brought Tan some of the fresh lemonade we made this morning," Molly said proudly. "Would you like me to pour you a glass?"

"Thanks, Molly, that would be great. But it sounds like Tan's the one who's been really working."

"Too hard," Hope said in agreement. "He didn't just

clean Desiree's hooves, he got all the girls fixed up. After you finish with that, Molly, I want you to head home and make sure he stays out of the sun until it cools off."

"Yes, ma'am." Once Molly poured the drink and set the glass on the kitchen bar in front of Lyon, who'd sat down on the first stool at the end of the counter, she began untying her apron. "Are you sure you don't need for me to wait with you until the fish are done?"

Hope shook her head. "No, since we bought throw-away pans, there isn't going to be anything to wash other than what you already did. Go and spoil Tan a little."

"I'll try," Molly replied, although she looked doubtful. "But he'll just spoil me more." She left the house shaking her head as though trying to resolve one of the world's most complex puzzles.

Hope pressed her hand to her heart. "Is that not the dearest thing you've ever heard? They so remind me of that O. Henry Christmas story, *The Gift of the Magi,* always putting each other first."

"Sounds like someone else I know," he murmured.

"What did you say?" Hope missed the first part of what he'd said and glanced back at him.

"I asked 'and how's Mommy and Biscuit?'" he added, nodding to the slight bump of her belly. It didn't show in her usual street clothes, but she was wearing a more fitted T-shirt this morning.

Hope got a kick out of his interpretation of the "bun in the oven" cliché. "Fine, though I did restrain myself to eating only one spoonful of the jalapeño stuffing, so the cooking smells are driving me crazy."

"You'll be like a rabid terrier before the picnic begins."

"That's better than being short stuffing for all of the fish.

As you can see, I was forced to use both ovens." She caught him stifling a yawn and was immediately concerned. "You didn't sleep well last night, did you?"

"Well enough."

"I think you should stay home and nap while I go to the picnic. After all, you have to stay up later to make sure everyone clears out safely after the fireworks display tonight."

"I'm not going to make you go to that alone."

"I'd miss you, but I'd feel better knowing you weren't jeopardizing your health—or safety." Lyon had been doing his share to make up for being short an officer since Chris Sealy got picked up by the Dallas PD. He and his young family had moved away two weeks ago and Lyon had been told by the mayor to delay hiring a replacement. Remembering that, Hope asked, "Any word on whether the city has removed the hold on hiring?"

Instead of answering, Lyon took a long sip of his lemonade.

The subtle evasion didn't fool Hope. "What aren't you telling me?"

"They're finally going to put my contract on the agenda for Monday's city council meeting."

"No!"

"So now you know why I didn't want you going to the picnic alone. I was hoping to delay you learning about that for as long as possible, and knew someone would be more likely to mention it to you if I wasn't around."

"Thank you for sparing me an ambush, but what about my right to hear it from you as soon as you got the news? Forget that." Hope circled the counter so she could put her arms around him. "Lyon, how can this be continuing when the autopsy report clearly vindicates you?"

"Your father's a stubborn old bull, you know that." He swung his chair a quarter turn to place her more comfortably between his thighs. "And our marriage has been sheer antagonism to him. Kent held him off as long as he could, but Ellis' man on the council is Dub Mooney and Dub is Ted Pettigrew's source for what's happening behind closed doors. Dub told Kent to either add it to the agenda or Ted was going to print an editorial about political subversion inside of city hall and go after *his* job."

They hadn't heard much out of her father lately, but Hope knew better than to think he'd been idle. "Dub can't get more than two votes against you," she declared after doing the mental calculations.

"Maybe not this time. But Ellis is patient. Next time it may be three, the next four. That's another reason for me to be visible as much as possible." His hands clasping her waist, he stroked her abdomen with his thumbs. "So next subject, please."

Hope wasn't as eager to move on. "You made me not want to attend."

"Don't say that. You know that would disappoint lots of people, particularly the seniors who just sit and watch and hope for someone to pause and give them a little attention. You're always very generous with them."

His suede voice and coaxing words took the edge off of her indignation and anger with her father. Sighing she hugged him tighter. "Thank you for reminding me there are more important things to focus on."

"Are you wearing that? Because if you are, the only thing anyone will be focusing on is how radiant and luscious you're looking."

Hope had been delightfully surprised herself at how

good she'd been feeling so far, and knew the pink-and-purple T-shirt's v-neckline was also exposing that she hadn't only rounded out a bit more in the tummy, but cleavage-wise, as well. "No, I'm wearing a patriotic tunic top with glitter and sequins. I'm not ready to announce anything until I'm through my first trimester."

"So this was all for my personal torment? Thank you."

"I'd planned to change before your return." Although there was a smile on Lyon's lips, Hope saw there was a slow burn going on behind those dark eyes and that made it impossible for her to ignore what that did to her libido and keep her own tone light. "Don't look at me that way."

"What way?"

The fact that he was willing to ante up the sizzle between them told her that he was disturbed about the upcoming meeting, too, and was in need of diversion. "Lyon, don't play with fire. You said it yourself—we have a busy day ahead of us."

"That's why I need a better hug."

Because of the entreaty she heard in his voice and yearning she saw in his eyes, she yielded to the hands that urged her closer. She knew what a risk it was and how the timing was all wrong. Painstakingly prepared food was expected…there were places to go…things to see to before that…but as soon as their bodies touched and he closed his mouth over hers, the desire that was never far from the surface short-circuited her ability to reason.

They had been navigating this sensual terrain with care, and yet not without a cost to their willpower. After weeks of living under the same roof, sharing meals and chores, they were growing more than comfortable in each other's company; their lives were becoming entwined—exactly as a married couple's should. Except that their unconventional marriage denied them the full, natural intimacy that would complete their union. Even the limited foreplay they assured each other was safe and helpful to ease sexual tension was having a counter-productive effect. It was evident in the deeper hunger of Lyon's kiss, and the intensity and possessiveness of his embrace. And when he slid his hands into her hair and all but feasted on her, she knew if he lifted her onto the counter, she would be hard-pressed to stop him.

With a groan, Lyon buried his face in the dark tunnel created by her hair and grazed the side of her neck with his teeth. "I've tried, but I can't stop wanting you."

And she wanted him. But the one thing that held her back was the commitment to herself that he could still get out of this union if he needed to. "I'm not being fair to you. Maybe you should…maybe if there's someone you're used to seeing—"

He recoiled as if he'd been struck. "Don't even go there."

"I'm being pragmatic," she entreated.

"We're married." Lyon looked so dumbfounded that he eased her aside and rose from the chair, paced several feet before fixing her with a stare as though she was suddenly a complete stranger to him. "I told you there was no one. Could *you* do that?"

"I'm pregnant!"

"And we're *married.*" With a harsh oath, he headed for the back door. "I need some air," he muttered.

Hope watched him go, miserable and torn. She really had trapped him into a life of a celibate monk with this arrangement. It was so unfair, so unfair.

* * *

Hours later as night fell and the town collected to wait for the fireworks to begin Lyon was still stinging from Hope's suggestion. He couldn't believe that she'd all but encouraged him to be with another woman. Like a barbed hook caught in his flesh, he could barely breathe, let alone move, without sharp pain incapacitating him. Did Will do such a number on her self-esteem that she thought all men were capable and willing to behave like that regardless of commitment or respect for her reputation?

It had to be the pregnancy doing something to her logic. "Pragmatic" his backside. She wanted him every bit as much as he wanted her—and he was on the edge of eaten up with it. What was holding her back?

He'd never seen her more beautiful and desirable than she was now, blooming with the life inside her. He watched her yards away sitting on a blanket with Kent Roberts' two kids, trying to keep them entertained while wife Shana gave the new baby a bottle. Hope was routinely dipping a long-stemmed wand into the container of soap and blowing bubbles that the children were trying to make land on their hands and arms like resting butterflies, then squealing when they burst. With her white sparkly top and her gleeful smile, Hope outshined everyone in his range of vision—even the stars. He didn't want this relentless ache in his belly, but he couldn't take his eyes off of her.

"We lucked out all around this year, didn't we?" the mayor said coming up beside him and leaning against his patrol car as Lyon was doing. "Just enough rain this week to keep the fire threat minimal, but not enough to make the fair grounds a disaster for parking and picnicking."

"Uh-huh," Lyon replied.

"It was still a good idea to spray for mosquitoes earlier in the week. Glad you suggested that."

"Uh-huh."

"Of course, I'd feel a lot better if that herd of feral hogs wasn't getting too close for comfort."

"Uh—" Lyon turned his head and frowned at Kent. "What did you say?"

"Just checking to see if you were paying attention." His old schoolmate matched Lyon's stance—arms and ankles crossed—and nodded at his family and Hope. "Marriage obviously agrees with her. I don't know when I've seen her looking better, and that's no empty compliment."

"Can't disagree with you," Lyon replied.

"Does she know about the meeting on Monday?"

"Yeah."

"You going to let her attend?"

Hope was her own woman. The idea that he could order her to stay away was nothing short of ludicrous, and the look he gave his friend said as much.

The stocky man with the wavy brown hair shrugged. "She's your wife. I figured there were some things Miss Independent would now be willing to defer to you on."

"How's that working for you with Shana?"

Kent rubbed at his whisker-darkened chin. "Good point. But then you're still on your honeymoon. Shana hasn't forgiven me for getting her pregnant again before the other two were out of preschool."

Although Lyon winced inwardly at the word "honeymoon," he replied, "Bet your Italian mother and grandmother aren't complaining." He so wanted to get the conversation off of him and Hope.

"Mom's bringing Grandma Lombardo back from Italy on Saturday. I may be *persona non grata* in my own bedroom, but at least my stomach will be pampered for the next few months."

Lyon knew Kent was kidding about any marital stress. Earlier he'd seen Shana watching Kent with the baby and her sheer adoration was impossible to miss. In contrast, he and Hope hadn't said ten words to each other since arriving here in separate cars, since she'd been right about his responsibilities and needing to linger after she would be ready to return home. Of course, that was his fault. He was the one who had been keeping his distance and when they did speak, his answers to her attempts at conversation indicated his lack of receptivity. He didn't mean to be curt, let alone rude, but he was also in no frame of mind to pretend he wasn't troubled and wounded.

"It's going to be okay, you know."

Although he knew Kent was referring to the council meeting, Lyon's thoughts lingered on his relationship with his in-name-only wife. "I hope you're right."

"Well, it's time for me to get this show going." The mayor slapped him on the back. "See you later."

As Kent made his way to the flatbed trailer where several bands and singers had been entertaining all afternoon, Lyon saw Hope close the bubble container and put it in one of Shana's two totes. Then she made her way over to him.

"This is quite a turnout," she said in lieu of a greeting. "Best we've had in a few years."

"We're almost not a rural community anymore."

"Have things been going well? I saw the ambulance rush to the pool area earlier.

"Did that teenager who hit the side of the pool with his ribs crack them?"

"Only bruised. The rest of the day has been okay. I'm sure we'll find some empty beer cans in the parking area later. If that's all, then we're doing good."

Lyon could feel her gaze on him but resisted looking down at her. If he did, he would be lost.

"Lyon, please don't be angry with me."

"I'm not." He wanted to be, that was the truth. Yet all he could manage was wanting her and aching because of it.

"I was only trying to be fair."

"What's more fair than being the man you need me to be?"

His quiet truth brought her hand on his bare arm and her forehead against the patch on his shoulder. He could smell her coconut shampoo and sugar body lotion seep through his senses and intoxicate him like a narcotic, but he didn't let himself touch her back.

As Kent took the stage and yelled, "How're y'all doing?" and the crowd erupted in cheers, Hope sighed and stepped back.

"I'm probably going to head home before the show is over. I'm more tired than I thought."

"Your cell phone battery still got a charge?" Lyon asked keeping his gaze on Kent.

"Yes."

"Okay. Take care and sleep well."

"You, too."

Freakin' fat chance, he thought in abject misery.

Chapter Six

By the end of the month, Hope knew two things: Lyon had almost forgiven her for what happened on the Fourth of July, and he still was Chief of Police of Cedar Grove. As a result, she should be as happy—or at least as content— as she'd been on July third, but it was now July thirty-first—Lyon's birthday—and nothing was going well.

She sat in Emergency at Cedar Grove General waiting on her father's doctor to report on Ellis' condition. He'd been admitted at eleven last night complaining of chest pains, and Hope had arrived shortly afterward when her father's butler, Greenleaf, called with the news that an ambulance had just carried him away. It had been a long night and thus far all she knew was that they were performing one test after another. Now it was almost seven o'clock and she'd hoped to be serving Lyon an extra special breakfast to start his thirty-sixth birthday off well. So far nothing else had helped to repair the chasm in their relationship. Instead she was sipping a diet soft drink because she needed the caffeine to stay awake, but her stomach couldn't bear one more sip of the tar they called coffee at the courtesy counter. Fortunately, she was the only one in the waiting room and didn't have to worry about making small talk when she least felt like it.

However no sooner did that thought pass through her mind when she heard the sliding doors open. Although he didn't look like he'd gotten any more sleep than she did, her insides melted at the sight of him, so handsome and official in his dark blue uniform. Belatedly, she noticed he carried a white sack.

"Hi," she said softly smoothing her hair and starting to rise.

"Stay put," he said. He set the bag on the coffee table, kissed the top of her head, and sat down beside her. "Any word?"

"Not yet." Hope felt a little dazed since that was the first time he'd voluntarily touched her in weeks. "They keep running tests."

"Maybe that's good news. If they'd found something, surely they would have told you by now."

"I hope you're right. It's so good of you to come, Lyon." She started to reach out, then checked herself and clasped her hands in her lap. She wouldn't make him uncomfortable, especially on his day. "Happy Birthday. I wanted to cook for you before you headed to the station, but—"

This time he kissed her silent. "It's a sweet thought, but don't worry about it. Did you get any sleep?"

"I rested a little here on the couch." She had folded up the blanket that had been given to her and returned it to the nurse over two hours ago. "Did you?" He certainly didn't look it. While appealing as ever and freshly shaved, his eyes were bloodshot and he had the same dark shadows under his eyes as she saw under hers in the bathroom mirror when she freshened up.

"Not much. I was worried about you."

He made her want to curl up on his lap and purr like a kitten. She had to look away until the burning threat of tears passed, then gestured to the clerk at Admittance, and to the security cameras. "It's perfectly safe."

"I meant worried about you and Biscuit being around all these sick people and not getting enough rest." He took both of her hands within his much larger ones and stared at that contrast as he stroked her with his thumbs. "The house has never been so quiet. It felt bereft."

That was not a tough-cop or football-jock word, but Hope knew Lyon used it with his own quiet truth because he was a reader. Not a latest *NY Times* bestseller aficionado, but someone who found moments in his life when education and experience had left him lacking in answers and he was seeking to fill those voids. Closing her eyes, Hope lowered her head until her cheek rested on his hands.

"Thank you." She could easily have fallen asleep like that—his warmth and strength her pillow.

"Don't get so comfortable that you go to sleep now, I'd be loathe to wake you up. Look what I brought you—your favorite French Vanilla decaf Cappuccino and a breakfast sandwich. You should eat while it's hot."

But before she could reach into the bag for the drink cup, Dr. Gandolf came around the corner looking more fatigued than either of them. "Hope...hello, Chief." He shook Lyon's hand and then focused on her. "I don't know what caused this episode. Let's get that out of the way first and foremost. As best as we can tell, he didn't suffer a heart attack or stroke, or angina attack. That's not saying that something isn't going on, but we'll have to get him to a different facility in either Tyler or Dallas for further testing to know for sure."

"But he was in pain."

Dr. Gandolf shrugged. "Maybe indigestion, although I listened to his stomach and there was no hint of distress there."

With a flash of intuition, Hope said, "He won't let you send him anywhere for tests."

"Well, then maybe you can talk to him because—"

"No."

"No?"

"Doctor, I believe you were right with your first guess. There's nothing wrong." Rubbing the kinks out of her neck, Hope gave the silver-haired, drained doctor an apologetic smile. "He pulled one over on you, Doc. He fooled all of us."

"You think? This is not something you play games with—and the bill doesn't come cheap, either."

"Make sure you tell that to the man who can buy you and all of your relatives several times over. I wouldn't blame you if you dropped him as a patient, but I'm telling you that the reason he pulled this is because he didn't succeed in getting Lyon fired earlier this month. He wanted to find out how willing I was to still come running if he wasn't well."

Vernon Gandolf shifted his gaze to Lyon, who shrugged and said, "It's possible. She knows him pretty well."

The weary doctor uttered a succinct reaction to that probability. "Okay, then if I can't get him to Dallas, I'll keep him monitored for another hour or so, and review my notes. If nothing changes, I'll have no choice but to release him."

"I'm sure you'll find him more than agreeable to that," Hope said.

Shaking his head Dr. Gandolf gestured for her to follow him back down the hall. "He's been asking for you every fifteen minutes since he knew you were here."

"I'll be there in a minute. Let me see Lyon out first."

As soon as the doctor was gone, Hope's slow burn intensified. "The nerve of the man!"

"Let it go. You've wasted enough energy on him," Lyon said. "I guess he's just running out of ideas on how to get me out of your life. Short of having me shot."

"Lyon! Don't even think such a thing."

He stroked her back. "At least you know that you won't be spending your entire day sitting here."

But so much time had been lost. "I didn't bake you a cake. You didn't get your present."

"You bought me a present?"

His bemused expression had her touching his chest in tenderness and reassurance. "Of course. I got you a hat and boots. I thought we could ride together sometime. I sneaked a peek into your closet for sizes because I didn't want to make a mistake." The last was a plea that he not get upset with her all over again.

"I don't know what to say."

"You're right, I should have asked for permission first."

"Hope." He lifted her chin so that she would have to meet his gaze. He started to say something, but instead leaned down and kissed her.

That communicated emotions that words couldn't. Hope let her body tilt into his, eager to absorb every sensation. How she had missed him and this, his tenderness and his strength.

Lyon was reluctant to sever their contact and lingered by touching his forehead to hers. "Are you going to be okay going in there alone?"

"Yes. I won't stay long. And I've already called Freddie to reschedule my meetings today because I didn't know what would be happening here."

"In that case maybe I'll take off early."

Hope loved how strong his heart beat against her hand. They made his words feel like a promise. "That would be lovely."

When he was gone, Hope collected her sack and went to find her father. He remained in an examination cubicle and didn't look happy about it.

"Took you long enough," Ellis grumbled as soon as he laid eyes on her.

"It could have been longer if I followed my first impulse to leave, once I realized what you'd done," she replied.

He shot her a dark look, but Hope remained unimpressed. He looked less threatening in that hospital gown. She did wonder, though, how they'd managed to get him in one of those. Probably only because he thought it would make him appear more convincing.

"What bull has that fool Gandolf been feeding you? He doesn't know what he's talking about. Can't recognize a sick man when he has one right under his nose."

His wild gesticulations sent the heart monitor going berserk, but although the nurses at the station were instantly alert, they didn't approach the cubicle.

"I'm sure he thinks your problem is nothing that the sight of an extra long hypodermic needle wouldn't cure." Hope didn't see an ounce of regret in his demeanor. "You should be ashamed of yourself wasting these good people's time. What if there'd been a real emergency here and you'd stolen priceless attention from someone?"

"Oh, stop the melodramatics. I don't have to listen to this."

"No, you don't. But you better have cried wolf for the first and last time. And understand this—" she took a step closer so she could keep her words strictly between the two of them "—you're not going to succeed in getting Lyon fired."

"We'll see about that."

"Then consider this—he's my husband. If he has to relocate, I'll go with him."

As she'd hoped, her warning left her father slack-jawed. Satisfied, she added with some reluctance, "Do you need a ride home or is Greenleaf coming to fetch you?"

Ellis ignored the question. Narrowing his eyes, he replied, "You won't leave. You're like your mother. You loved this place too much."

Although his pronouncement held its own shock, Hope managed to avoid flinching. But in that instant she did think him a particularly warped human being. "If that's the only reason you managed to keep her with you, I'm more disappointed in you than I can say. No wonder you thought I'd marry Will if he'd survived. But you're wrong about me. Maybe if Mother had lived you would have found out you were wrong about her, too."

Without waiting for a reply or to see if he did have that ride home, Hope left. She had to believe that her father was speaking from a point of loneliness and selfishness and didn't really believe what he'd said about her mother. It had to be terrible to have a lover and partner gone for so many years already. Maybe he was starting to feel abandoned by her. All she knew was that a year ago his surgically sharp words would have debilitated her; now she rejected them and returned to the property with a sense of excitement. Lyon had changed that for her.

She should have been exhausted, but as soon as she got home she was energized, and a luxuriating bath only added to that. Molly arrived shortly afterward and Hope had her starting on the cake while she blow-dried her hair. Then she put out Lyon's gifts on the breakfast table and helped Molly with the icing.

After the cake was on the racks cooling, they went outside and picked the garden. Although Lyon wasn't a fussy eater and seemed to like everything she'd made so far, she knew there was nothing like a thick, juicy steak dinner. The steaks were out on the counter defrosting, while a marinade was mixed together waiting in the refrigerator. Hope collected tomatoes, bell peppers, and had Molly retrieve the last of the hanging spring onions from the awning by the garden shed. They never used chemical fertilizer, but everything was still washed well and left to air dry in the dish drainer to go with the store-bought organic lettuce, since it was already too hot in Texas for lettuce to grow until October, when temperatures dropped permanently from triple-digit threats and even the 90s.

Once they had the cake frosted with a homemade mocha chocolate icing and chocolate shavings, Molly returned home and Hope checked in with Freddie again and returned some calls.

She was cutting zinnias and day lilies for a bouquet for the breakfast nook table when Lyon returned. It was just after three in the afternoon. Feeling as light-headed and hopeful as she did on the day of their wedding two months ago, she met him in the kitchen.

"Five minutes and I would have had these in water and

everything would have been perfect," she told him as he unbuckled his gun belt.

"I'll leave and come back," he said. He even did the side-to-side dart reminiscent of his old football days when he'd been Will's favorite receiver.

"No!" He might be teasing her, but she was taking no chances. "Come sit. Can you have a beer before you look at your presents?"

"I'll get it. You go ahead and try making those flowers look prettier than you."

Hope had changed into a gauzy poet's shirt that showed off her sun-kissed complexion to perfection. She could still wear her jeans, but they were low rise and she had to leave the top button open; however, the shirt hid that.

Returning with the beer he whistled at the cake. "You and Molly have been busy."

"A little bit, but I suspect they already OD'd you on sugar at the station, huh?" she asked.

"Hardly. I got a foot-long hot dog for lunch with a card that reads 'Dream on,' several other cards far worse that I won't describe or ever let you see, and we'll leave it at that."

"Ruthless bunch you work with."

"They're enjoying tormenting me about you whenever they get the chance."

"Because I'm Ellis Harrell's daughter?"

"Because you're the most beautiful woman most of them have ever seen, a little younger than they think I deserve and any one of them would have stuck a fork in my thigh to beat me in a race if getting you was the prize."

"Did I say brutal? I meant twisted."

"They're okay." He took a long drag on his bottle and sighed with pleasure. "The sign at the bank is reading 105.

I was going to suggest we go over to my family's farm so I can check on things and feed the horses, but you don't need the heat or the rough drive on the four-wheeler I keep there."

"But I'd like to see your horses. And you could start breaking in your hat and boots."

He looked pleased. "You're sure?"

"Let's give it a shot."

Lyon walked over to the table and looked at the boxes. Hope realized he was looking for a card, but she'd skipped that part of things, stuck on what the right tone should be given his reserve lately. After all, "To my darling husband" would have hardly fit how things stood between them.

Thankfully, he soon opened the hatbox and smiled at the beautifully woven summer hat with the rattlesnake-skin band and turquoise-and-silver buckle holding it in place. He whistled silently.

"That's a beaut."

He slid it onto his head with the casualness and confidence of a man well used to Western hats and would have had Tan mimicking in hero worship. Hope watched with the pleasure of having remembered the shape of the one he'd worn since he was helping his father on the farm; she'd managed to get the fitter her father always used to duplicate it.

The boots took a little more work to get on, but also fit like they were made for him. "I can't wear these on anything but pavement dressed in my good suit," he said in concern. "It would be criminal to make them dusty or muddy."

"It's not like we're going to be tromping through any lowland," she said delighted that he was thrilled with them. "Why don't you change and I'll pack some bottled water?"

Lyon stopped her as she turned to get the canvas tote in the washroom storage cabinet. "This is more than generous. More than I deserve," he told her.

"No, it isn't."

"Yes. Considering the way I've been acting—"

She rose on tiptoe and kissed his chin. "Happy Birthday, Lyon."

He started to reach for her, only to check himself. "I'll go change," he said.

Having missed his touch as much as their conversations, Hope felt a slight pang of disappointment; but she took heart: at least this was a step in the right direction.

Less than fifteen minutes later they were en route, driving Lyon's silver Chevy extended cab pickup truck, which he kept parked on the far side of the driveway since he'd moved in. Hope had offered the use of hers, but the farm had a dirt driveway and he didn't see a reason for her clean truck to get dusty.

"What did your father say?" he asked as he adjusted the air conditioner.

Hope didn't want to ruin the pleasant atmosphere they'd been enjoying but didn't see how she could refuse, so she relayed their conversation to him. As she feared, he didn't like what he heard.

"He's no better than a bully," he muttered.

"You wouldn't be in a very good mood, either, if you'd gone through the battery of tests he did."

"He wouldn't have had to endure them if he hadn't lied. You're the one who suffered standing watch all night and worrying. I'm sure that did the baby a heckuva lot of good, too."

"The baby has the best bed in the world," Hope countered stroking her tummy. Sighing she continued, "I'm not making excuses for him, but he's an empty, unhappy man."

"Mostly a result of his conduct and choices in life. Splitting us up would magically change things? Now that's twisted."

Hope enjoyed the scenery and let him vent. She'd done her own share in years past.

"Do you think your mother would have left him in time?" Lyon finally asked.

"If he'd spoken to her that way, it's possible. But he didn't. He was tough, yet ultimately he always could be tamed or toned down by her. Like I said, she's been gone too long and without her good influence, he's gone rogue."

As they turned into Lyon's family's farm, Hope looked at the remnants of where the house once stood. He'd done a great deal of cleaning up since the tornado. There was a new barn and a small trailer where he'd stayed on weekends when he was doing major projects that kept him working past dark and waking at dawn. The oak trees on the place were over a century old, but there were few of them. That's why the tornado had kept its strength and been so deadly.

"Is it hard to come back?" she asked.

"Sometimes. Does it bother you?"

She could see that he was sincerely concerned and shook her head. No one enjoyed going to a funeral home or cemetery, and coming to this site where loss had taken place brought its own vibrations. However, she felt no malevolence here, not like one would at a crime scene.

"It does make me sad for you," she admitted.

"That's why I haven't stayed in the trailer in a good while. In the last year I've been feeling my aloneness too much when I'm here."

Since about the time that she had gotten engaged to Will. Was that a coincidence? The thought made Hope's pulse leap.

Lyon parked in the shade of the barn and his two geldings, Big John and Dodger, left the shade of the nearest oak and wandered lazily over to them. Lyon brought out the bag of apples he'd sacked at the house and began slicing pieces for them. John wasn't the largest horse Hope had ever seen, although his withers stood inches higher than she did, but his attitude made you think he was. He made sure smaller but wily Dodger waited his turn for the treats and still sized up Hope all at the same time. He pawed the ground several times before he let her get close and stand next to Lyon.

"I'm honored, Big John," she said finally stroking the seriously alpha horse.

"Don't take it personally, you're quite a mystery to him," Lyon explained. "He hasn't been exposed to a female in some years and your scent combined with that of the mares' on your clothes intrigues him." He, too, stroked the snorting horse's nose and told the proud animal, "Behave. I know you're eating up her attention as much as you're salivating over the apples."

Dodger was all charm and mischief, at once skirting around Big John to appeal to Hope for his own TLC, then nipping at John's rump to get his attention off the treats so he could get his share. Invariably, he would have to dart out of the way of the larger horse's bared teeth.

"It may be hard to believe, but those two are usually good pals," Lyon said. "They're just showing off for you."

"Didn't you have some cattle?" Hope asked scanning the rest of the property.

Lyon pointed over a low bluff on the west that hid the pond and a larger grouping of trees. "They're probably staying close to the water and shade. I only keep about twenty head at a time. That's enough work for one man, although Tan said he would like to help out. Your few half-grown calves don't exactly fulfill his hunger for working with beef critters."

Hope laughed. "I suspect I'd better get more land fast."

Lyon got out the four-wheeler and gave her a slow and easy tour of the place. The cattle were exactly where he told her they might be. The pond was churned up to more resemble a mud puddle indicating they recently indulged in a dunking.

"The flies are getting bad," Lyon noted as the cattle swished and slapped their tails, then stomped their hind legs to chase off the pesky insects, especially from udders sweet from milk and sensitive from growing calves' teeth.

"Thank heavens for civilization so women don't have to go through that torture," Hope said wincing in sympathy. She caught a secret smile tug Lyon's firm lips and lowered the sunglasses she'd put on for the ride to give him a warning look. "Don't even think of going there."

"But it's my birthday."

It was wonderful to see his eye light with amusement and his broad chest shake with secret laughter. Except that her imagination went into overdrive, too, and that had her breasts growing taut and ultra sensitive to where the delicate satin and lace was unbearably uncomfortable. She slid her hands between her knees and clamped them tight to keep from fidgeting.

As they circled back toward the barn, Hope eagerly tried to change the subject. She pointed to the area behind the great oak where Big John and Dodger had returned. "If you were ever to rebuild, that would be the perfect spot for a house. There's not a good view of the road, but that grouping of cedars around your north property line would be a great wind barrier against the winter cold, and the oak would protect from the summer storms." She couldn't help but remember the tornado that had killed his parents and three others in town, as well as injured several more.

Lyon slowed to consider that. "I hadn't given it much thought, but you're right."

"Then again, you might not want to rebuild." She didn't want him to think she was suggesting that *he* live here again.

"Not for myself, no," he said. "I thought of putting up a house and then listing the property with a Realtor. I'd definitely have to if I was forced out of my job. But I guess I automatically thought of the existing home-site location, only there's no slab there, so you're right. I could build elsewhere, and your idea is a good one."

He circled away from the barn and stopped near the old home site. The surviving shrubbery that had once circled the house had gone wild and looked like the entryway to a secret garden. Lyon pointed to an open area. "That's where I found them. My mother was pulled from the house, then crushed by debris. My father survived long enough to crawl to her. He lay there with his hand covering my mother's. That was all of her that he could see."

Hope had heard something to that effect, but had never broached the subject not wanting to bring back the painful memories. "Everyone who has mentioned them always spoke of them as having a true romance until the end."

"You're right. I was always a little envious of them. Proud, but wondering where I went wrong."

Sliding over to him, Hope laid her head against his shoulder and her hand on his thigh. "Don't do that to yourself. You're on your own timetable."

Weaving his fingers between hers, Lyon squeezed gently. "You think?"

She could feel his melancholia as weighty as the heat. As still as it was there was barely enough air to breathe, and Hope swallowed as a droplet of perspiration trickled between her breasts like a lover's touch, another down the small of her back—unwanted stimulus when they were this close. Her breath shuddered as she exhaled and that drew his attention.

"It's too hot for you."

"I'm all right."

Clearly not convinced, Lyon drove back to the barn and parked the four-wheeler, securing it behind padlocked doors. Hope waited for him near the barn entrance. She leaned against a support beam and created an artificial breeze by fanning the hem of her gauzy blouse. A fluttering caught her attention and she looked up to see a pair of doves entering the barn and settling on the rafters to complete a mating dance they'd obviously started outside.

"You can't wait one more minute?" she muttered.

"Guess not." Lyon joined her, a wry smile curving his lips. He put his arm around her shoulders and led her to his truck where he opened the passenger door for her. As she climbed in and sat back against the seat, she gasped in pain and immediately leaned forward.

"What is it?" Lyon asked.

"Something stung me."

"Turn around, let me see."

"Ouch! It did it again."

She did and he lifted her blouse several inches and swiped his hand along her lower back.

"An ant," he said. "You must've picked it up while leaning against that beam. Hand me an ice cube from that tote bag on the floorboard. That should give you some relief and keep you from scratching and making the wound worse."

Hope pulled off her glasses and gave him an arched look over her shoulder. "Pain or no pain, you're not tormenting me with any ice cube!" She began to sit back in her seat, only to squirm and tug on her shirt. "Oh, blast—now my imagination is kicking into overdrive. Lyon, check and make sure there aren't any more crawling on me."

"Good idea. When has there been just one ant? Hold still."

She did as he directed sitting ramrod straight as he lifted her blouse even higher than before and brushed at the inside of the material. But when he did the same to her back, the strokes grew slower, until they were undeniable caresses.

"God, you have lovely skin," he murmured.

"Thanks. Did you—did you find any more?"

"No, although when I brushed the material I'm sure if anything was there it got knocked off. Do you want me to check your front?"

After a brief laugh, she said, "Nice try." But when she turned back to face him, she saw there was no amusement in the eyes shadowed by the brim of his hat. There was only raw desire. Her overactive libido needed no further stimulation and Hope dropped her gaze to the snaps on his light denim shirt. "Seriously, I'm sure I'm okay now."

"Are you?"

Two little words and yet spoken by Lyon they held a powder keg of meaning and emotion that had her trembling as though he'd just slid his hands under her blouse again.

"Hope…are you having one of *those* moments?"

She could have her own 1-900 number for what was happening inside her. But all she could do was nod in misery.

"Look at me."

That was so not a good idea, and yet she lifted her gaze to his anyway.

"Come here, sweetheart."

Bless him for understanding, she thought and with a sigh of relief, Hope wrapped her arms around him. Their initial body contact had her shuddering due to her body's aroused state. "This is insane," she whimpered. "I've loved being pregnant except for this. This is torture."

"What did your doctor say?" he asked, his breath tickling her ear.

"Ms. Helpful, you mean. She said it wasn't a problem, it was a gift, and to have all the sex I wanted. Hilarious, isn't it?"

"She doesn't know about us?" he asked stroking her from her hair to the small of her back.

"No. Lyon, that's our business, no one else's."

After a few seconds, Lyon said, "I think you should consider following her advice."

Somehow she'd known this would be his reply. "How can I? How fair is that to you?"

"It's not as though I wouldn't be getting something out of it."

Hearing the smile in his voice, Hope leaned back and met his concerned, compassionate gaze. How like him— he could find the humor in something like this and still understand this wasn't funny for her. She so wanted this. Him. If only he felt—or rather she wouldn't feel…

"Would it be easier if I decide for myself?"

She nodded.

Lowering his gaze to her lips, he said, "Don't end up hating me for this."

Then he tilted his head and closed his mouth over hers. When their tongues touched, she moaned with pleasure.

What started out as a tender probing soon grew intense as layer after layer of reserve and restraint yielded to repressed hunger. Hope couldn't hold still. Her hands had a mind of their own, at once clenching at his shirt, then wanting to explore the texture of the hair at his nape. His back muscles reminded her of her equestrian days when her highly trained mount's muscles flexed and strained as they flew over hazardous terrain during the cross country part of the competition.

Groaning, Lyon lifted her from the seat only to lean her against the cab door, and trapped her there with his body. "Wrap your legs around me," he said against her mouth. "I won't let you fall."

She had no doubt about that; she was worried about climaxing before he kissed her again. It was impossible not to be aware of how full and sensitive her breasts felt crushed by his chest, or how his arousal so perfectly fit against her core. If they'd been naked, she wouldn't have needed further foreplay; she was that moist and ready for him. Her mind showed her how it would be behind her tightly closed lids as he moved against her again and again matching the rhythm of a kiss gone out of control. And when she climaxed, he did, too, and they absorbed each other's whimper and moan just as they'd shared this incongruous ride.

Hope's body continued to hum with the passion he'd stirred in her, but finally, slowly, Lyon let her lower her legs to the ground. He didn't let her go altogether, though and they stood forehead to forehead panting as they waited for the world to stabilize beneath their feet.

"I thought that would take the edge off, but it didn't, did it?"

His voice sounded as dry as her throat felt. All she could do was manage a single negative shake of her head.

"We could go home," he added, his gaze holding hers. "Try again."

Hope had to moisten her parched lips. "I need a shower first."

"Me, too."

With that decision almost a palpable thing between them, Lyon drove back to her farm. He handled the truck as though he was carrying a load of nitroglycerin. They made no pretense at small talk, and yet it was clear that they'd never been more aware of each other.

Back at the house, Hope exited the truck with care upon discovering that her legs were still weak; she felt as though she'd been riding for hours. If Lyon could have that potent an effect on her after just a little heavy petting, what condition would her body be in when they truly became lovers? As a new wave of heat turned her forehead damp and cheeks hot, Hope blotted at her brow with the back of her hand.

Lyon came up beside her and slipped his hand under her hair to gently stroke the back of her neck. "Okay?"

There was a good chance that she would never be all right again. She was both excited and a bundle of nerves, but with an affirmative nod, she said, "Sure." She was determined to win some control over herself. That's the woman Lyon was used to seeing—calm, cool, collected Hope.

Once inside she set the canvas cooler on the kitchen bar.

That could be dealt with later. "Meet you back here in a few minutes?" she asked.

"Yeah, I'd like a drink. I know you can't have anything, but can I pour you a glass of juice or a soft drink when I get out?"

"There's peach tea in the refrigerator. That sounds good."

Lyon nodded then lightly stroked his thumb over her swollen lips. His Native American blood made it difficult to grow a beard, but her skin was so fine that what afternoon whiskers he did have had marked her. "I'd better shave again, too, because I'm damn well not done kissing you."

Calm, cool and collected...calm, cool, collected.

As Hope headed for her shower, she repeated that mantra over and over in her mind. What a fraud she was.

Lyon stood with his hands braced against the marble wall, his head thrown back willing the cool spray to ease the fever in his body. Ice chips as sharp as razors could have been shooting from the shower head and he doubted he would have felt them, nor would they have changed his condition. As long as his mind was on Hope, he was going to stay aroused. So be it, since there was no one and nothing else he would rather think about.

Her response to him had at once awed and humbled him; he'd never been with a more passionate woman—and they hadn't had intercourse yet. The way she'd clung to him with that elegant body, the way she'd whispered his name just before she'd climaxed as though in prayer had sent him over the edge, too. Heaven knew he was praying to be what she needed, all that she would ever want.

Shutting off the cold water, Lyon toweled off and eased into a fresh pair of jeans that he left unzipped for comfort as much as practicality. The white shirt he slipped into was left unbuttoned, as well. He'd already shaved so there was nothing left to do but go make that drink. His mouth was beginning to go dry in anticipation of what would follow— not that he needed any stimulant to make love with Hope. If anything he needed to slow down the flow of adrenaline in his body. He could not fail her.

He was only on his second long sip of a scotch and water when Hope emerged from the other side of the house. Already impressed with how quickly she'd achieved this transformation, her black spaghetti-strap sundress—constructed of just enough material to melt what was left of his ability to reason—had him putting down his glass to keep it from slipping out of his hand.

"Happy Birthday to me," he murmured.

She laughed softly. "I'm glad you like it. It's so much cooler. I should have worn this to your farm."

Hope had never flirted with him before; back in her Will days, that wouldn't have been right. Now, she didn't have to, her power over him was so strong that he was captivated by her. Nevertheless, he liked that she thought she needed to seduce him—and wanted to.

"If you had worn that," he replied, "we'd still be there."

She crossed to him, barefoot as he was. With that crazy Mocha-whatever nail polish, her feet were as pretty as her hands, and that dainty toe ring with the heart charm on her right little toe was ridiculously sexy, the impact of it going directly to his groin.

Feeling his tongue thicken, Lyon spared himself conversation by handing her the tea she'd asked for. Thanking him with that secret smile that drove him crazy, she took a long drink.

His own drink forgotten, he admired the graceful curve of her neck and the way she filled out the bodice of the empire-waist dress. Hope was no air-brushed magazine photo and was proud of it. He was simply and utterly grateful. "Want me to check your ant bites?"

"Only if you're prepared for what I'm not wearing underneath this." Her gaze slid over his exposed chest and belly, lingering at the gaping V of his jeans. "I'm glad we think alike."

He couldn't let her keep tying him into a sensual knot or he would explode just standing there. "Then you won't be disappointed if dinner is delayed?"

Slipping her left index finger into a belt loop on his jeans, she replied, "Come with me and you can atone."

As a seductress, she was adorable and he would have been well on his way to falling head over heels if he hadn't been living in that Purgatory for years. Now he just waited to show her that having freed him, his universe would forever begin and end with her—if she wanted it that way.

In the shadowy bedroom, beside the turned-down bed, she stopped and faced him again, this time slowly sliding her hands inside his shirt and inching upwards over his hard abdomen, his taut nipples, next caressing him with her breath, then her lips as she slipped the shirt off his shoulders. Sucking in a sharp breath, Lyon stroked her hair and watched with masochistic fascination as she duplicated those delicate ministrations to his right side, until he was forced to stop that sweet torture by framing her lovely face with his hands and urging her head up to receive his kiss of gratitude and ravenous hunger. He was determined to be patient and attentive, learn what else she liked and how many ways there were to bring her to the ecstasy he wanted for her. But he was only human.

"You feel so good." He drew her closer until the silk separating her feminine curves from his hot flesh was irrelevant. Her nipples were like sharp little needles tormenting him and, as he plumbed her mouth with his tongue, he ran his hands up and down the outer swells of her breasts, then reached between them to score the hard little points with the rougher pads of his thumbs.

"Lyon," she breathed. "Can't we lie down so we can feel all of each other?"

"First let's take care of this."

He slipped one strap off her shoulder, then the other, until the black wisp of fabric drifted to the carpet and she stood before him an exquisite, honey-skinned angel of temptation. The gentle swell where her child grew made his heart pound with barely containable emotions and he sunk to one knee and brushed a tender kiss on her flawless skin. "Little mother…"

"Lyon."

There was a hitch in her voice and his hands were a little unsteady as she stroked his hair. When Lyon rose he saw her eyes were over bright and dreamy. She'd never been more beautiful to him than at that moment.

"You, too," she urged her hands already at the waistband of his jeans.

Lyon shoved them to the floor and stepped out of them, achingly aware of her unabashed gaze.

"I'm glad that I can see how much you want me," she said slowly lowering herself onto the bed. "You've always been something of a mystery to me. So self-contained. Now I get to know at least one secret."

Stretching out beside her, stroking her from shoulder to hip, Lyon replied, "You'd be disappointed if you knew how few there are."

She reached down and closed her hand around him. "I don't believe that."

Having been flattened by three-hundred pound line-backers, kicked bloody by unruly cattle, and once even finding himself looking down the wrong end of a .12 gauge shotgun, Lyon didn't think there was too much that would make him beg for anything including his life, but this small woman with her fantasy body and sweet soul could. He knew it in that instant as she slid her leg over his hip and brushed his feverish length against her moist softness.

"Believe this," he said rolling her onto her back. Concerned not to crush her, he raised himself on his elbows and finished what she'd started. Thankfully, she was caught up in the same intoxicating cocktail mix of time-place-person as he was. Wet and hot as sin, when she tightened her inner muscles around him as tightly as she did her thighs, he knew this sharing was doomed to be over quickly, too. What saved his pride was recognizing that's exactly how she wanted it.

"Look at me," he rasped. When she did, he began moving inside her. "I want to see your eyes when it happens for you. I want you to know it's me."

She stroked his forearms and biceps the way she had his more sensitive muscles and raked her nails over his chest like a kitten flexing her claws. "I know it's you."

His muscles beginning to twitch from the sweet hell she was inciting in him, he asked, "I'm not hurting you?" He looked down at her so much smaller than him and that fragile little swell of her tummy, barely visible as she lay on her back.

"You won't...and the baby is well protected."

In the end it was her emotional discomfort and physical

need that allowed him to break a personal vow. All night, he had to remind himself. They had all night.

Lowering his head, Lyon promised as much to her. "All right, sweetheart, hold on."

Chapter Seven

Waking alone in the middle of the night with the room cast in a light as though there was a full moon outside had Hope spreading her arms wide across rumpled silk sheets and striving to remember if the soreness that came with well-used muscles and the images that flashed before her were real or was she caught up in a dream? Either way her bed was empty. Lyon was gone.

As the drug-like thick weight lifted a bit and her mind started to clear, she knew with certainty that the moon was in its final cusp and couldn't be so bright, and that she and Lyon had made love. *Three times?* Four if she counted that little appetizer at the farm. Because that had led to this, she most definitely would.

Shifting again to find his scent on the pillows beside her, she sighed as her body telegraphed sensations to her mind, surfacing memories of his exploration of her. Just as he was a man apart from others in his work and as a friend, he'd proven to be so as a lover. She'd learned there was much in him that was old-fashioned. *Traditional,* she amended, sensitive to the male ego. He was fair, poignantly generous, but even in his lovemaking reluctant to give up total control. She knew his work had forced him to see the worst sides in human nature, but who had made it difficult for him to trust a woman he took to bed? What woman had wounded his heart that he hid his vulnerability at the very instant his life's seed was pouring into her?

Hope opened her eyes. She was pregnant. She was the only one with whom it was safe to have unprotected sex. That would have made it all the more intense an experience. And yet he was gone. Why had he returned to his own bed?

Saddened, Hope buried her face in his pillow and soothed herself by stroking her only companion left in the room. Poor baby. Now she remembered. For an instant as Lyon began to climax that first time, he'd opened his eyes and she'd seen his total awareness that the baby she was carrying wasn't his. There had been a flash of pain in his dark eyes, and then he'd hidden it again and was all concern, all generosity.

Because despite everything, he wants you.

Wants being the problem. It was wonderful, of course; but it wasn't enough. Dear Lord, she had been a naive fool to think it could be, just as she'd believed helping to keep Lyon in Cedar Grove would be adequate penance for her stupid mistake with Will. Owning Lyon's gratitude was a reward for sure. But she wanted more. She wanted his love.

Oh, where was he?

Brooding about his whereabouts wouldn't help her to go back to sleep, but that didn't stop her from wondering.

Belatedly, Hope realized the light in the room was coming from another part of the house. And wasn't that talking she'd heard just now?

She slid off the bed and, on her way to investigate, grabbed an ivory cashmere throw off of the chaise lounge at the foot of the bed. Wrapping it around her shoulders, she continued out of the room, her bare feet almost silent on the wooden floor.

There in the lavender-blue glow of a plant's growing light, she found him standing naked, looking like some Sci-Fi movie's mouth-watering alien-who-fell-to-earth. With all that was going on, she'd forgotten to plug in the light, but he apparently had done it needing the added illumination to help operate the phone now held to his ear. Hope stood transfixed, admiring his broad shoulders, firm buttocks, and powerful long legs.

"Not at all, you did the right thing," he said to whoever it was that was on the other side of the connection. "Right, take it. You know where the keys are. Don't worry about it. Try to get some rest and I'll see you later."

Closing his cell phone, Lyon turned and saw her. His expression turned regretful. "I tried to be quiet."

"You were," she said coming to him. "I woke because I missed you." Parting her wrap like a butterfly spreading her wings, she then closed it around them both.

"Did you?" he murmured his tone as pleased as his expression.

With his erection pressing all the way up against her diaphragm, she managed a breathy, "Oh, yes."

Smiling ruefully, Lyon lifted one strong shoulder in a resigned shrug. "You'd think it would have developed some discipline in the last several hours. But then it's your fault for coming out here looking more incredible than anything I could dream."

Instead of an inadequate "thank you," Hope touched her lips to his chest and felt his strong-beating heart. "Did something happen at the station?"

"Cooper Jones had a spinout on one of the back roads trying to avoid a feral hog and her litter."

"Is he all right?"

"He's in better shape than the sow and three of the eight in her litter. But his SUV is scrap metal. I told him to take the patrol car that Chris used to drive."

Hope winced at the thought of the ugly scene. Those horrible creatures were nature's marauders, tearing up the land—when they weren't ravaging family pets or causing traffic hazards like what apparently had happened to Lyon's detective. Glancing at the microwave and stove clock, she frowned. "What's he doing working at almost eleven at night?"

"He's not. It happened at dusk. He was doing some follow-up work on an old case after hours. The exciting life of divorced cops," Lyon added with a sardonic twist to his lips. "It took him until now to get a wrecker out there and then to get his forensic bags out of the SUV and back to the station."

Hope couldn't help but think of repercussions, her protective instincts toward Lyon kicking in. "The expense of a new vehicle won't endear you to the city council."

"It'll be cheaper than a huge hospital bill if he'd been severely injured."

"Don't expect our fair-and-balanced local press to think that way. By the time Pettigrew finishes describing the accident, it will somehow reflect on you. You know it will."

Lyon stroked his free hand down her back to soothe her, but it became a sexual caress as he lingered over her bottom. "I never realized you were such a mommy. You can't worry over every little thing, especially as it relates to me and my job. Not when you have so much on your own plate."

How like a man—invincible and self-reliant prior to a tidal wave or hangnail. "Women come out of the womb multi-tasking. You never ate!" she declared immediately, proving it as she realized that she'd passed out from exhaustion and she never did make him that scrumptious birthday dinner.

"I ate. I feasted," he amended. "Breast of angel, leg of vixen…"

"If you say butt of Bambi, I promise somehow or other you'll hurt for a week."

Laughing, Lyon swept her up into his arms. "You do have a delectable tush. But the truth is that I ate a chunk of my birthday cake while waiting for Cooper to sign some forms for the wrecker driver. Sorry for the caveman table manners, but the cake is terrific. Did Molly help you?"

"Stop changing the subject, and put me down. I can have your steak in the broiler and be scrambling some eggs to go with them in nothing flat." But before she finished with that suggestion, they were back in her bedroom and Lyon was laying her on the bed. He trapped her there with his body. As good as that felt, Hope still protested. "Lyon, this wasn't the birthday I planned for you."

"Have you had the night I wanted for you?"

Despite the darkness, there was enough light that she could see his face grow somber. She laid her hand against his cheek. "You need to ask that?"

Lyon took that hand and planted a kiss in her palm. "I'd like to be sure before I dare ask to spend the night."

Was she that hard to read? "If I hadn't wakened, for all I know you'd still be here."

"That was the plan. Follow the strategy of a throw-away pup who lays low hoping that he won't be noticed and kicked out into the cold."

The comparison of a desperate, lonely pup to his superman self was laughable, but Hope couldn't bring herself to tease him. Come daylight, reality would burn off this sweet magic that protected their false marriage quickly enough. Where was the harm in lingering in this fantasy world for a little while longer—or as long as he was willing?

"Stay, Lyon," she said quiet but serious. "It feels good and right with you here." Glancing over his shoulder she added less confidently, "That closet on the left in the bath suite is empty, too. You could put your things in there so they would be closer."

It wasn't poetic or close to what she wanted to say, but at least she felt him relax beside her.

"Would you also let me spoon you while we sleep?"

We. The word filled her with something as poignant as when he'd slipped his ring on her finger. "I might. I don't know," she replied giving him the honesty the moment called for. "Is that actually comfortable? I've never been spooned before."

She sensed a dozen questions spawn, and then percolate inside him. Although his eyes grew troubled and a frown formed decisively cutting a lightning bolt line between his dark eyebrows, he voiced none of them, for which she was grateful. But slowly, with breathtaking tenderness, he eased his arm around her waist, then slid his body flush against her back. When he gently slid his left leg between hers, the rest of his anatomy voided any pretense that the night would be an ode to sleep and the recuperative powers of rest.

His breath was warm on her nape, his lips were hot against her skin when his teeth lightly scored her shoulder. The scent of chocolate had Hope licking her lips in anticipation.

"It's not only comfortable," he told her. "In some locations it's vital to survival."

He made her feel so protected and wanted that she closed her eyes to cherish this simple moment of sheer bliss. "I can see how this might make up for a shortage of fur pelts in cold climates," Hope said, dutiful student she was willing to be.

But when he slowly, carefully slid himself into her receptive body, Hope closed her eyes at this primal, yet natural way of tethering female to male. Nothing man could invent could compare with such a complete sense of well-being.

"Lyon..." she sighed.

"Yes, my dream?"

It was the last thing she remembered saying to him. The next thing she knew her clock was beeping her awake, and Lyon was already showered and making her coffee in the kitchen. What did or didn't happen remained a mystery to her, but his mysterious smile kept her blushing for days afterward.

When the promise of fall came in September, Hope's pregnancy advanced to where questions were impossible to avoid. Even so, she was carrying the child so high and totally in front that from the back she didn't look pregnant at all. The first time she ran into someone she hadn't seen in a while, the startled look on his face when she turned around to acknowledge his presence was priceless. It happened at a Dallas charity event and the gentleman in question just happened to be one of the men her father tried to match her up with right before Will had proposed to her.

"Hope." The tall, dashingly attired man kissed her on both cheeks in the European fashion that people in his circles emulated with enthusiasm. "I didn't realize congratulations were in order. I saw nothing in the news and Ellis didn't tell me."

"I'm not surprised. How are you, Reed?"

"Fine. Crushed to find you more of a vision than ever, but I'll muddle on, dawdling tortoise that I am."

Reed Ames was no dawdling anything. A real estate tycoon still in-between wives number three and four, he was old enough to be her father, but a gentleman in the way Golden Era film stars were heralded for their deportment. His photograph was regularly on newspaper society pages everywhere. Suspecting that this time would be no different, Hope reminded herself to warn Lyon in case that photo included her and not the dazzling blonde who had arrived on his arm an adornment like some men wore diamond cufflinks and expensive watches.

"When is the baby due?" Reed asked.

"Late winter or early spring," she replied resorting to her most vague answer.

"Who's the lucky father and—" Reed's eyebrows arched as he examined her left hand "—mister?"

Focusing on the unspoken "husband," Hope replied honestly, "A lovely man. You don't know him, but don't speed if you come driving through our neck of the woods anytime soon."

"It took a uniform to win your hand? I'm going to buy myself a yachtsman's jacket tomorrow."

Not everyone was as gracious. A week later at Cedar Grove's *Day to Give Back* event where residents were encouraged to take the initiative to clean up yards that had become an eyesore in town, paint someone's house that either couldn't manage or couldn't afford to do it themselves, see to repairs where needed, or fill in for those who were short-handed in help, Hope was helping register animals at the pet-dipping vaccination tent at the city park. Two women who could certainly afford to take their toy poodle and Maltese to a groomer came up to register their pets for a free bath and flea-tick dipping. It was impossible for Hope to miss their smirks and blatant stares at her stomach as she worked in her increasingly snug red T-shirt. But she kept her smile intact as she signed in the eight animals in line before them.

"Aren't you the one who was engaged to Will Nichols?" they demanded when it was their turn to register.

"What can I help you with, ladies?" she asked.

"It is her," the other insisted. "My…look at you. Are you having a boy or girl? You know Rochelle is pregnant, too, only she's definitely bigger than you are. You must be carrying a girl because she's carrying a boy."

Hope kept her eyes down to prevent them from seeing her shock. "Can I have your dog's tag number for ID and your name and phone number, please?" she asked in her most business-like voice.

"How long a wait will it be?" the owner of the Maltese asked.

"As you can see, we have a great number of dogs in need. Some of them are seriously contaminated with fleas and ticks," she added in a stage whisper.

The owner of the poodle stared distastefully at the large tubs of treated water. "They do change that for each bathing and dipping, don't they?"

"Well, they do the best they can," Hope replied seeing a way of ending this humiliating experience. "I'd be sure to spray my clothes when I got home to rid myself of any infestation, and then wash them with bleach." She was going a bit overboard, but the ploy worked. The women quickly abandoned the line and their agenda on behalf of Rochelle.

Hope didn't feel guilty for scaring off the troublemakers, and assured the disapproving woman taking the donations beside her that she would make up the lost revenue herself. The wife of a Baptist church deacon, the older volunteer had heard enough to judge Hope guilty of something, if only bad taste in her connections, and wanted no contamination by association. She didn't speak to Hope again for the rest of the day.

As for the suggestion that Rochelle was pregnant and that the baby was Will's, Hope felt strangely apathetic. Will was fast becoming a sad mistake in her life and any results of those days were more the Nichols' business than hers.

It was a relief to be relieved by another worker and Hope continued around the park encouraged by the cooler but pretty weather. The cheers and applause from the big tent drew her attention. That was the wine and art auction, the proceeds being split between the town's library, food bank, and animal shelter.

A local DJ was acting as emcee and was luring more onlookers than there were tables and chairs, already claimed by Cedar Grove's most affluent. Despite her somewhat haggard condition after the long hours outside of the pet tent, Hope joined the outer rim of observers and was scanning the crowd when her eyes locked with Summer's. The ever-colorful forty-something divorcée was resplendent in the season's latest fashions. Hope bet that outfit would be returned to the rack at her store by morning and the sales tag reattached bearing the full price amount. Next to her, Hope's father was no shy mouse, irreverently dressed in white although it was weeks past Labor Day. A matching Western hat, pearl gray ostrich-leather cowboy boots and an obnoxiously large cigar completed his ensemble. When Summer pointed her out to Ellis, her father's gaze chilled as he focused on her stylishly form-fitting T-shirt. Without so much as a nod in acknowledgment, he turned away. Openly thrilled with his visible censure, Summer gave her a saccharin sweet smile followed by a "whatever" shrug and turned back to the auctioneer, too. Hope was used to her father's ways, but his letting Summer give the illusion to others around their table that she had tried to get Hope an invitation to join them was more than Hope could stomach. The final straw in the offensive day came as she found Summer bidding against her for a landscape painting by a local talent. The price had gone up to where she knew Summer would never risk her own money confirming her suspicion that this would be a gift from Ellis to his paramour. Summer failed in her plan, but it cost Hope twice what she felt was a fair price for the painting.

She was putting her purchase into the trunk of her car when Lyon pulled up behind her. He shifted into park and stepped out to inspect the painting.

"Nice," he said after a too-brief kiss hello. Except for a few waves and wistful glances from across the park, this was the closest they'd been to each other all day except when they'd dressed and he'd whistled at her scooped-neck top that showed off her improved cleavage as it did her pregnancy's progress. Then he'd buried his face against her and swore evening could not come soon enough.

"So this is what you were telling me that you wanted for the mantle for Thanksgiving," he said studying the painting. "This cropping of trees looks familiar to me. The artist is a nature-lover for sure. The wild turkeys can be that plentiful, but you have to be patient and wait for them to get over their skittishness."

She should have been pleased with his approval; instead, Hope found herself stinging after all from all that had happened today. "Ellis gave Summer permission to bid against me. My own father."

Lyon took a philosophical perspective. "That sounds like one of his tactics. Then he still makes things look like he helped charity. Forget it, sweetheart. You know he enjoys stirring things up for his own entertainment. And if he sees that he can get under your usual reserve with a woman who uses brighter eye shadow than most transvestites, he'll do it again."

True, but Hope wasn't in the mood to be reasonable right now. "*And,*" she sniped back, "Rochelle Sims is pregnant." Her annoyance with him was irrational as it was unfair. He would have to be a mind reader to know the real reason she was upset, but that didn't stop her.

She felt Lyon's gaze on her profile and knew he was waiting for more—particularly an apology. Hope hated conflict and went out of her way to avoid moments like this. She also knew that he was wondering when the day would come that she could stop thinking of Will and how much of a fool he'd made of her. It wouldn't be today. If he were alive, she would have unlocked her .12 gauge shotgun from her safe, driven over to the Nichols ranch, and emptied every shell into his dually.

"Is this where I'm supposed to ask who sired the poor thing? Because, frankly, Hope, I don't really see the point at this stage even if it is Will's."

So wrong an answer.

"The point is that what was once just a bad-joke rumor looks now to be the ugly truth. Do you think I want my child to know he has an illegitimate brother or sister virtually his own age?"

"I thought you had decided this was *our* baby?"

Hope clapped her hand over her mouth. She'd said it that way, hadn't she? When trying to convince Lyon that he should marry her. "Lyon, I'm sorry. Don't listen to me. I should just shut up and go home. That was just shock and hurt speaking."

Before he could answer, Lyon's radio triggered. He clicked the speaker he had tucked through his shoulder epaulet, but his gaze remained on Hope. "Teague, over."

"Chief, we have a situation in town. Disgruntled diner put his chair through the front window of Sally's Home Cooking."

Watching Lyon turn into the left-brained machine, Hope wondered what could have happened at the warm and friendly restaurant. Someone off of his meds, she surmised.

"Has he been contained? Any injuries?"

"Juarez has him. A kid on a skateboard was passing by at the same time and has some nasty cuts. Paramedics are on the scene stabilizing him for transport to the hospital."

"I'm on my way. Out." Wearily rubbing his face, he gave Hope an enigmatic look. "I have to go."

Feeling totally shut out of his mind and heart, Hope wrapped her arms around herself. "I hope the boy's injuries aren't severe. Be careful," she added inanely.

"There'll be statements to take and make, and paperwork." And they were still shorthanded.

"I don't know when I'll get through," he concluded.

He stumbled slightly with "through," which told Hope that he had intentionally avoided saying "home," a term he used with visible pleasure since moving into the master suite with her. That made her want to go after him as he headed back to his patrol car and wrap her arms around him until he understood her. "Lyon," she entreated as he paused and glanced at her over the roof. "I truly am sorry."

"I know. But it's what we say when we don't intend to that says the most about how we feel."

The disappointment flattening his voice hurt as much as his reluctance to hold her gaze, and he quickly climbed into his patrol car and drove off. Lucky man, she thought. He could escape her. How did she escape herself?

She had single-handedly brought an end to an idyllic few weeks. He had even been planning to go with her for the ultrasound in three days when she would hopefully be finding out if the baby was a boy or girl. This couldn't be the flip side of those raging hormones, could it?

Nice try, Hope. Wrong is still wrong.

Knowing it would be impossible to return to the festivities and pretend all was well, Hope returned home. The sun was sinking fast on the horizon and the air was progressively cooling, but she dreaded the idea of spending the next hours cloistered in the house surrounded by Lyon's possessions and scent when she knew how precarious she'd made things between them. After carrying in the painting and placing it on the mantle, she cut up some apples and walked out back to visit with the mares thinking maybe that pleasant task could distract her.

Desiree, the gray alpha female, was the first to spot her and trotted over with expectant enthusiasm for her share of treats. Black, mellow Bella, who liked to lay her head on Hope's shoulder to where you couldn't tell where her mane ended and Hope's hair started was heaviest with child and came more slowly. Saucy, the Dun, was the daintiest and least likely to behave with or without treats. An eye-catching gold with a white mane, she was mindful of Desiree's jealousy and impatience with her, but skirted around to get an apple slice at every opportunity.

Once she was out of treats, Hope walked over to the remains of the vegetable garden. She regretted not having had the time for a late-season garden this year, but promised herself that she would do better by spring. The baby would be here and they both would need the exercise and the fresh air.

Deep in thought, she failed to see or hear Saucy trying to sneak around Desiree, but apparently Desiree didn't and the incensed horse charged. Whether she meant to keep Hope's attention for herself or worried there might be one slice of apple left, the gray slammed into Saucy, who spun around screaming. She inadvertently struck Hope with her hind quarter knocking her off her feet as though she was nothing more than a bowling pin caught in a perfect strike.

Striving to catch her balance, Hope's aim was inches off and, instead of stopping the fall, she raked her left hand and wrist over the sharp edge of the garden's corner t-post and the overlapping cattle panels they used to keep the animals out of the plants. Hope knew even as she landed that she'd done more than scratch herself. Confirming that was a shout from far off. By the time the first blinding pain dimmed enough for Hope's vision to clear, she saw the horses were dashing away as Tan came chasing across the pasture yelling like he was performing a solo rendition of Pickett's Charge with a leaf rake held high instead of a rifle topped with a bayonet.

After her second attempt to get to her feet, she saw Molly was quickly catching up to him in their pickup.

"I come, Miss Hope!" Tan shouted as he neared. Then he went into a slew of Vietnamese that Hope thought sounded like a slew of kittens protesting as they were being dumped from a barrel. She didn't identify one of the half dozen words she'd learned from him so far.

"It's okay," she lied holding her abused arm against her belly as she bent at the waist and kept her balance by bracing herself against the cattle panels. She didn't care if the blood ruined her clothes or not. She'd already decided that she could never wear the thing again without being reminded of this awful day. "I just need to wash up and bandage it."

"Need ER," Tan enunciated carefully as he arrived beside her. Hardly breathing as she expected, he gently but firmly took hold of her arm to inspect the long, ugly wound.

Joining them, Molly was momentarily at a loss of what to do or say. "You—you need stitches. Tan stitches himself, but I think you need too many for him to do it."

Hope didn't need that visual in her mind what with her stomach going from queasy to openly in attack. One thing she knew for sure, she wasn't leaving here. "I'll settle for some disinfecting and pressure bandages," Hope replied.

"Call Chief," Tan directed his wife. "Maybe baby hurt."

Shuddering at the mere thought, Hope reassured them as she did herself.

"No," she said stroking her tummy with her good hand. "Things feel fine there, and Lyon is very busy with someone seriously injured in town today. Let's not add to his troubles."

Accepting that the Lees would not give up until they were convinced she was all right, she let them help her into the house and assist her in the clean up and wrapping of her hand and wrist. By the time it was done, under Tan's direction, Molly had her looking like she was preparing to be the understudy for the remake of The Mummy.

While Tan went out to make sure everything was secure outside and the mares corralled for the night, Molly warmed up a cup of homemade chicken soup for her.

Once she convinced her that all she needed now was rest, Hope got Molly to leave, too. She was tired, depressed, and totally disgusted with herself for getting herself into the predicament of letting herself end up between two argumentative horses. She knew too well that you never assumed anything with an animal regardless of how fond they were of you, especially when the critters were larger than some of today's hybrid automobiles.

She had been dusty before the fall and felt all the messier now. She should have asked Molly to stay and help her get undressed, but in the end, she had no reservations about taking scissors to her shirt. Once it was slit open like a gutted fish, she stripped out of it and the rest of her clothes. Getting her hair clipped on top of her head wasn't too difficult thanks to today's broad variety of hair accessories, and a plastic shopping bag served as adequate protection for her bandages from water.

A long soaking bath would probably have done her more good, but Hope was afraid once she got in she would fall asleep and sink underwater. She got into the shower, she got out of the shower and, once toweled off, she collapsed into bed unable to summon the strength to bother with a nightgown.

Despite her protests not to, she began to hope that Tan or Molly did phone Lyon. But she fell asleep with a heavy heart knowing he would not come if he could.

It was nearly dark when Lyon drove into the garage. He was so tired and wired that he almost over-accelerated instead of braking, then he had to punch the garage genie three times to make it descend behind him. That was warning enough to get a grip before heading inside to face Hope.

Staying put and seeing things through in town had been the hardest thing he'd done since challenging his mortality against the flames burning up Will's truck. When Tan called with the news about the horses and Hope's injury, he had wanted badly to brush everything and everyone aside and race home, especially since Tan hadn't been all that clear or reassuring at first. But being right in the middle of that fiasco at the community hospital, Lyon knew leaving would have been the equivalence to handing his badge away for good. Then what help would he be to Hope?

Tan had finally assured him that things were under control and that the bleeding had stopped, so he had been forced to put Hope's well-being on an emotional back-burner. But that had been over two hours ago—when Tan and Molly had been officially ordered home by Hope. It took only minutes to bleed to death, and from what Tan had told him, the worst of her cut had come extremely close to her most vital artery in her wrist.

Once inside, Lyon's devil's advocate kicked in stronger. It was so dark. That just wasn't right. Hope liked either the plant light or the stove light on. If she knew he was running late, she would leave some of the accent lighting on, then later tweak down to the subtler lights. Wasting no time on hunting for buttons or plugs, he flipped the nearest switch and the room blinded him with fluorescent brilliance. Thinking that enough to see to every corner of the house, he made his way to the master suite.

The stark lighting didn't wake her but he could see her clearly asleep in the bed. She looked so still and pale, and her injured hand lay across his pillow as though she was searching for him in her sleep. He didn't see any sign of blood coming through the bandages that mummified her from the beginning of her palm to above her wrist, but the amount of area covered made his stomach twist as hard as when he'd first heard Tan's voice on that incoming call.

The laceration had been *that* long?

He needed to see. Tan had some basic first aid knowledge—Lyon had inquired about that weeks ago after Hope had confided in them that she was pregnant—but that held less stock with him now when she suddenly moaned in her sleep. She was clearly feeling pain. And a wound that large would undoubtedly scar her permanently.

Feeling sick at heart, he eased down on his side of the bed. Yes, she was hurting; a small frown kept trying to etch a line between her eyebrows. Was that because of her hand alone, or was something going on in her womb?

He would go quickly and at least wash his hands so he could check her for fever and monitor her pulse. But before he could make good that intention, her lids lifted and he found himself looking into her eyes.

"You're home."

"Yeah." His voice sounded unfamiliar to his own ears and he cleared his throat. "How are you feeling?"

"Not great, and none too bright. You can save the lecture or brow-beating, whichever was the plan. I've already given myself several renditions of both."

The impulse to do either had vanished the instant he'd entered the dark house and thought the worst. "That's some bandage."

Hope glanced over at it as though that part of her anatomy belonged to someone else. She probably did wonder because she was careful not to move it.

"Overkill. The only reason Tan and Molly stopped was because they ran out of antibiotic ointment and gauze."

"That's not what I heard." Tan also assured him that he had come into town to restock on bandages and such while Molly had kept an eye on her.

Grimacing, Hope averted her gaze. "I should have known Tan would call you."

"You think I gave him my business card months back just to help him get out of a ticket?" When she briefly closed her eyes and compressed her lips, he knew she was feeling another throbbing or spasm and he wanted badly to sweep her into his arms and absorb the pain for her. Instead, he asked, "When did you last have a tetanus shot?"

As the moment passed, she opened her eyes to study the three-tiered ceiling. "Two years, six months and…I forget how many days ago. I'm safe."

"Being a wise guy isn't going to make me go away any sooner."

Her look was sheer confusion. "Why would I want you to do that? What I was saying was that's when I inadvertently ripped off half of this thumbnail." She held up the right one that had since grown back perfectly.

This time it was Lyon's turn to close his eyes. "How in heaven's name did you do that?"

"I'm not a princess, Lyon," she said with some indignation. "I did help create a good deal of what's around here. My nails get dirty. Sometimes I hurt myself."

He was upsetting her and didn't mean to, but didn't she see? They were married. She was his wife, and maybe the child wasn't biologically his, but it was his nonetheless, and she had to let him be upset and worried for her, for them, whether it was rational to her or not.

"I'm not trying to pick a fight," he said quietly.

Her gaze flicked to him, then away. "I tried to apologize. Now I'm scared and every time I open my mouth I seem to be making it worse."

On the contrary, it was getting a little easier to breathe. He had thought they'd experienced something earlier today that would make him lose everything that they had begun to create together. He didn't ever want to experience that feeling again.

"That boy in town?" he began sharing the other tiny slice of hell he'd lived in this afternoon. "His mother immediately threatened to sue the city as well as the idiot, who wouldn't restrain his emotions. Sue despite the ordinance against skateboards on the sidewalks—and you know what? I can't say that I blamed her. So I couldn't leave until the boy was out of danger and I talked the mother down from her hysteria in order for Kent to speak with her. The town isn't out of the woods yet, but the father finally arrived from a business trip out of state, and he talked with her, too. What you need to know is," he concluded searching her face as though memorizing each feature anew, "during all of that and watching how easily it is to have everything in the world and then almost lose it, I was worried sick about you. I don't know how much longer I could have stayed if the father didn't arrive when he did."

"Don't say that." Turning on her side so she could reach him with her good hand, she caressed the faint pink scars that remained on his ear, then brushed the backs of her fingers against his whisker-roughened jaw. "I'm proud you stayed. No one understands how hard it can be to do the right thing than you do, Lyon."

They sat there letting their words heal them, and bond them closer.

Finally with a sound of regret Hope added, "I overreacted about Rochelle. And I shouldn't have let those two women get to me."

"That would have been a good trick considering that they ambushed you."

"Whatever. The thing is that under normal circumstances Summer's behavior wouldn't have been a blip on my radar."

Lyon took hold of her right hand and touched his lips to it. "I know that. About Rochelle's news…do you think it's possible that the baby is someone else's besides Will's?"

"Clyde and Mercy will certainly be hoping so."

When their gazes met again, they burst into laughter. Just as quickly Hope gasped.

"What?" Lyon started to reach for her bandaged hand and then checked himself. "Do you need a pain pill?"

Hope stared at him, her eyes wide, her mouth a perfect

O. Silently, she pushed the sheet down past her waist, took hold of his hand and laid it on her stomach.

"Hope...sweetheart...what's wrong?" When she didn't immediately answer, his dread grew. "Don't do this to me. Are you cramping? I'll get a blanket and take you straight to the hospital."

"Ssh. Wait!"

Wait for what? he thought fearing the worst. Then he felt a bump beneath his fingers. "Whoa!"

Hope grinned through her tears.

"Oh, my." He had just witnessed a miracle and couldn't take his eyes off of her. "Biscuit's got quite a kick."

"You should feel it from this side of things," Hope mused.

Something quieted inside Lyon and he relaxed and stroked the spot over and over. "Do you think it'll happen again?"

"I suspect so."

"I shouldn't be doing this," he said as reason replaced wonder. She looked like a porcelain figurine, too perfect for him to touch. "Look at me, I need to shower."

"But I wanted you to experience this with me."

He met her radiant smile. "Is it the first time?"

She nodded.

When it happened again, he grinned like a fool. "That one wasn't as strong. I bet it's getting tired. Too much exercise for the first day." Filled with spiritual grace and unfathomable tenderness, Lyon drew the sheet back up over her. "You have to keep it warm."

Visibly tiring, Hope managed a chuckle. "You can't keep calling her 'it.'"

"Why are you calling her 'her'?" She couldn't know which she was having since the ultrasound wasn't happening for days yet.

"I've been praying while waiting for you to come home. It helped to ignore the deepest throbs." Her expression reflected both embarrassment and hope. "It struck me that it would be a blessing if the baby is a girl."

"I don't understand."

"It would be easier on you."

Easier for him to accept? Lyon was as blown away at her concern, but wondered, too. Didn't she realize that any tiny life that came from her body would be precious to him?

Unable to resist, he leaned forward and gently kissed her. "If she is a girl, I hope she's a perfect miniature of her mother."

"Gallant answer."

He kissed her again, but then forced himself to rise before he started to cry. "What can I get for you before I head for that shower? You have to have something for the pain, you were practically sobbing in your sleep."

"No, I'm afraid to. I don't have anything in the house except aspirin and acetaminophen and I've been reading that one can cause bleeding in the baby as well as me, and the other can cause wheezing in newborns. Imagine, simple over-the-counter drugs! I'm not taking any chances."

But Lyon could tell by her eyes that it had been and would be an ordeal. He only knew of one way he could help, minimal though it was. "Then I should go sleep in the guestroom," he told her. What if he accidentally bumped her during the night? They'd been together long enough now that his body automatically sought contact with hers even in sleep.

Hope looked instantly stricken. "Please don't. It would help having you close. We could switch sides."

Lyon eyed the queen-size bed. "There wouldn't be enough room for your arm to stay isolated like that."

"There would be if you spooned me."

Tempting as that—as well as the seductive look she gave him—was, he knew the extent of his own endurance. "We always get in trouble when I do that." Just the thought of her sweet bottom pressed into his lap stirred him to life.

"There, you see?" she coaxed. "The best kind of pain relief. Especially since Tan advised me to take off my ring because my fingers were starting to swell and he was concerned it would cause circulation problems. But now I can't even stroke it to pretend you're near."

Lyon had been unconvinced until she said that. She had just admitted to doing something he did all the time when they were apart. "Let me go get cleaned up," he said in surrender. "You scoot over."

Chapter Eight

On the first Tuesday in October, Hope and Lyon sat in the waiting room at Dr. Jacqueline Winslow's practice. They were her last appointment for the day, which gave them the privacy Hope had wanted for Lyon, since he hadn't had time to come home and change out of his uniform. They might be in the next county, but crossing county lines to transact business was a common matter in this sprawling state and one never knew who knew whom and would report a man in uniform from a distant town.

"Nervous?" he asked her as she reached over and gripped his hand.

Hope knew he had purposely positioned himself on her right so that they could do this. Her left hand no longer needed a bandage, but it remained sensitive. At least she was able to get her ring on again, she thought happily, fingering it with her thumb.

"I didn't think I would be, but I am." She rested her head on his shoulder. "It's not as though there's any pain involved."

"Good. Because you couldn't ask me to stand there and watch if there was."

He kept his voice low so that his words were for her ears only and Hope loved the way his breath caressed her hair. "But you've already signed up to be my natural childbirth coach," she teased.

"Under the condition that you understood I might not be able to go through with it on D-Day."

"B-Day," she amended, not at all worried.

"Stop being adorable when there's nothing that I can do about it in here."

Hope was giggling as the door opened and a nurse said, "Mrs. Teague?" She bounded quickly to her feet. "That's me."

To her surprise, Lyon held back. "Is something wrong?" "Do you want some time alone first?"

"Don't be silly," she replied tugging his hand. "You know my body better than anyone here. Besides, with an ultrasound, all I have to do is raise my blouse."

"Thank you for sharing," Lyon replied, trying to ignore the smirking nurse.

Jacqueline Winslow was a tall, slender woman of forty with cropped blonde hair and kind gray eyes. She hugged Hope and shook Lyon's hand.

"Well, this is our big day, isn't it?" she said slipping on her gloves.

"One of them," Lyon muttered.

Hope grinned at her doctor. "Can you tell that we've been discussing the natural childbirth classes?"

"Is that what I was sensing between the lines?" Dr.

Winslow shook her head in bemusement. "It never fails that some of the strongest and bravest dads-to-be turn into Jell-O at the first sign of our mommies going into labor."

"I'm going to take that as confirmation that instincts still have value," Lyon drawled.

Hope shivered as the doctor put the cold gel on her stomach. "Sorry about that," Dr. Wilson said. "You'll get used to it in a second—or to be more accurate, totally forget about it. Watch that screen," she added placing the transducer probe onto the goo. She started easing the probe around, paused to type in some adjustments on the computerized part of the machine, then moved it some more. "Here we come…ah, and listen to that heartbeat. Best sound in the whole world until Delivery Day."

"D-Day. Told you so," Lyon said under his breath.

"Smarty," Hope replied, her gaze locked on the screen. Then her mouth fell open and she squeezed his hand even tighter. "Oh, my Lord! Is that her? I can't believe it." She had to blink furiously because tears were threatening to blind her.

"Her?" Dr. Winslow continued with her scanning. "It's a little late to put in an order."

"I know." Hope sighed. "But can you tell?"

"As a matter of fact, she's being very obliging this afternoon. I don't know how you knew it, but Mommy and Daddy had better start thinking of little girl names."

Hope dropped her head back onto the pillow and laughed with delight. "Thank you!"

Dr. Winslow reviewed Hope's chart with her, answered the questions Hope had brought with her, and gave her the contact information for the classes. The nurse printed a copy of the baby's image for Hope and also presented her with a DVD, too.

Hope was still staring at the picture as Lyon drove them home. "Isn't she beautiful?"

When Lyon didn't immediately reply, she turned to look at his profile in the dimming light of dusk. He'd been so quiet for the rest of the session. She thought she caught him gulping once, but with her own compromised vision, she couldn't be sure. That would be wonderful if he was as moved and thrilled as she was. Much stayed an unmarked road ahead of them. The most important things remained unsaid. That made it scary when she thought too far into the future, so she tried not to except when clients and black-and-white issues demanded it.

"She's going to be more than beautiful," Lyon said at last. "She'll be her mother's daughter. A single word won't ever describe her."

He always managed to move her with his simple yet almost romantic reflections. Why was she worrying?

Because *I love you* was simple and romantic, too.

She reached over and gently touched his nape. "Are you okay?"

"Watch the hand."

"I'm watching," she replied knowing full well what he was up to.

She accepted that he was going to make the most of Dr. Winslow's scolding; she knew it as soon as Jacqueline had spotted her injury and learned what they did not do that night. Although the wound had scabbed over and seemed to be healing, the doctor had demanded that if anything like that should happen again to get to the ER immediately. She spoke two words to make Hope realize her potential folly. "Staph infection."

In this day and age when germs could not only ignore

but outmaneuver state-of-the-art drugs and mutate, Hope had risked having a safer, healthier pregnancy. She'd learned that she was wrong to assume that being current with shots and careful with hygiene and medication that she was protected. And there was a danger of MRSA, which her doctor explained as "methicillin-resistant" staph bacteria. As a precaution, Dr. Winslow had the nurse take a blood sample to make sure there was no sign of infection in her bloodstream.

"I'm okay," Lyon said with a misleading nod. "Provided I can lock you in a safe place for the next four months where you only get out when I'm home to watch you."

"The concern is touching," she said playing along with him. "But what a caveman concept for such a respected women's advocate. Can't you see Pettigrew's headline? *Pregnant Sex Slave Discovered in Police Chief's Closet.*"

"I'm not talking as a law officer or the chief law authority. I'm talking as the concerned man in your life."

Hope looked out the passenger window at his careful phrasing. How could they be so free and open with each other when alone—particularly in bed—and hit this indescribable, unmovable mental glitch when it came to their public persona as a unit? Why not "husband and lover?" Was it because lover had the word *love* in it?

"I know you worry," she said this time touching his thigh.

"I like your doctor."

"Jacqueline lost her own baby and husband in a car accident ten years ago. She never remarried, but she adopted a special needs child."

"Lucky kid." Lyon folded his right hand around her fingers avoiding her palm that retained subtle swelling.

"Would you like to stop somewhere to eat? To celebrate? It would save having to fix something at the house."

"Are you hungry?"

"Not really, I had a late lunch. But if you are, I'd find something and keep you company."

"I had a big lunch, and—" with her right hand, Hope plucked at her red-and-black maternity top "—if you don't mind, I'd like to get home and wash off this gunk. The wipes the nurse gave me don't cut it."

"I had no idea. Of course."

They did reach home less than an hour later. It was dark and the lights that Lyon had set to come on by various timers since Hope's accident were working as programmed, lending a welcoming glow inside and out of the sprawling house.

As soon as they were in the kitchen, without even taking the time to remove her shawl or put down her purse and the DVD, Hope fastened the sonogram picture to the refrigerator with the service-number magnet from the side. "Ta-da!" she sang to the little being in the picture. "Your first piece of refrigerator art."

"Be careful what you wish for." Coming up beside her, Lyon put his arm around her. "Today a mesmerizing printout, tomorrow a wall-papered appliance—like a kitchen doesn't lend itself to being a fire hazard in a dozen different other ways."

"You cynic," Hope said laughing and threatening to punch his shoulder. "I bet your mother treasured your school drawings." She couldn't wait to see glimpses of what was going on inside her child's mind. "When I was growing up," she said to make Lyon understand, "the refrigerator was Mrs. Crandall's property. Don't get me wrong, she was a good woman, but she didn't want scribbles of stick figures with purple hair and eyelashes that resembled tarantula legs marring her everything-in-its-place territory."

"Poor rejected artist."

She supposed it must seem silly to anyone else. "How would you feel if your work was tucked away out of sight in a file?"

He gave the question about three seconds thought. "Confused. My stuff was used to start stove fires. Productive little guy that I was, I was instrumental in keeping us warm all that winter. After that I quit drawing and took up building ship models. They don't burn as well and the smoke stinks. I found out trying to have a Viking funeral in our stock pond. My dad gave me an earful when he came chasing out there thinking the pasture was on fire."

Hope gave him the arched Alessandro stare that Lyon recently told her made him almost hear flamenco music. "If you had said model horse kits, I might have believed you."

"Sissy stuff."

"You seriously did that?"

"Heck, no, there was no money for that. As soon as I was old enough, I got a paper route to start saving for college because I knew there was no way my parents were going to be able to afford to send me."

"Now that sounds like the Lyon Teague I know," Hope said over her shoulder as she moved on to the bedroom. She set her purse on her vanity in the bathroom, and folded the shawl and laid it on a shelf in her closet. As an afterthought, she slipped off her heels. They were low in comparison to what she was used to wearing, but they, too, made her back ache as if she wore them all day.

When she reemerged, she saw that he was removing his gun and the belt with the extra clip, and putting it in his closet. "I'm sorry that you had a demanding childhood."

He shrugged. "It kept me fit and taught me discipline. Let me help you with that." Coming up behind her, he moved her hair aside to unzip her top.

"Thanks." Hope watched him in her vanity mirror. "I guess we do need to start thinking of girl names."

Startled, he met her gaze in the mirror.

"What?"

"Well, I thought you'd want—" He shook his head. "Hope is what I would pick."

She made a face. "I like my name, but it would feel a little egotistical."

"Why?" Lyon scoffed. "Men do it all the time with the junior and second, third thing. It's a badge of honor. Let's get that left arm out of the sleeve before this knit material gets caught and rips off some scab prematurely."

"How lucky am I to have my own personal dresser," she said softly as she watched him focus diligently on his task.

"The official un-dresser." His secret smile suggested he enjoyed his own humor. "How about Rebecca Hope?" he added finally lifting the whole top over her head.

"Close!" She was delighted that they were almost on the same track. Watching as he laid the top on the edge of the garden tub, she said, "I was thinking Meredith. Meredith Rebecca Teague."

She watched as Lyon stared at the back of her head and then met her eyes in the mirror. "Our mothers would like that," he said quietly.

"I think so, too. I like the way Meredith flows off the tongue. It also makes me think of the lilt in inquisitive children's voices. You'll probably hate this, but we could call her Merri while she's little."

Lyon's eyes lit with humor as he took gentle hold of her shoulders. "Hope and Merri...doesn't that pairing demand it's own photo Christmas card?"

Dropping her head against his shoulder, Hope looked up at him. "Oh, you!"

She saw desire change the light in his dark eyes as he realized that she was wearing the red-over-black lace bra that had made his chest rise and fall the first time he'd seen her in it. Hope hadn't yet done more than finish unzipping her low-rise jeans but his glances down into that V indicated that he knew she had on the matching panties.

Framing her face with his right hand, he said, "Meredith or Merri, I can see I'll be quickly outnumbered and outvoted."

"No, you won't, but thank you for agreeing."

He stroked her high cheekbone with his thumb. "How could I not? I ache just looking at you," he said before lowering his head.

His kiss was possessive yet tender, hungry yet generous as he strived to give her as much pleasure as he was taking. When Hope reached up to slip her right hand to his nape to deepen the kiss, he groaned and gave her what she wanted, stealing her taste and then her breath with his tongue. Locked in this sensual prison, he slid his hands down her arms and over her breasts. Her sheer bra immediately exposed her arousal and he intensified it by circling her nipples, then raking his thumb nails over the ultra-sensitive peaks.

Hope's sounds of yearning abruptly ended in a choked cry and her body shuddered with the sexual need that remained close like a prowling predator whenever they were within sight of each other. Murmuring something she couldn't discern, he then slid his right hand into her jeans until he cupped her.

Her body jerked, defenseless against her own passion. When he drew her harder against his hips, it exposed the answer to an unasked question. Yes, he was as turned on as she was aroused.

Hope wanted to turn and wrap both arms around him, but she wouldn't even if she *could* free herself from his sensual vise. She would only get that awful gel on his uniform. As it was, he was probably getting some on his sleeve, but she could no more warn him than she could stop rocking against her hips in the erotic, age-old rhythm he coaxed from her with his hand.

The more the tension built, the more feral the bite of her fingers at his nape and the wilder his kiss. Then he tore his mouth from hers and with his teeth on her neck groaned in a quaking climax that thrust her into sensory overload, and she gasped from her own release.

Lyon wrapped both of his arms around her, clutching her to his chest and rocked them soothingly until his heart didn't beat like a jackhammer against her spine and neither of them was still panting like marathon runners.

"What you do to me," he said, his face buried in her hair.

Hope leaned her head back against his shoulder. "I want you inside me."

"In about five minutes," he said. "As soon as I shower." He kissed her hair before releasing her to start unbuttoning his shirt. "Come with me?"

Hope chuckled briefly. "Don't look at me that way. You'll get my hair drenched and I only washed it hours ago. Then you'll be lying in bed asking me what's taking so long to dry it."

"Not if you'd stand where I could watch you." He tossed his shirt beside hers.

"By the time I finish," she said ignoring that, "you'll be twenty minutes into REM sleep."

Glancing down at himself, Lyon muttered, "Want to bet?"

As he opened the shower's frosted glass door to turn on the spray, Hope turned away to the vanity to turn on the sink water and adjusted the wand to a comfortably warm temperature. Under her lashes she watched Lyon strip off the rest of his clothes. No, it wasn't likely that he would be asleep quite so soon. His provocative invitation and his own active imagination had sabotaged him. He may have climaxed two minutes ago, but his body was in denial.

As he closed the door behind himself, Hope exhaled a not-quite-steady breath and quickly stripped out of her lingerie knowing that he would waste no time in there. Reaching for the fluffy white wash cloth, she saturated it in the hot water and pumped some liquid coconut-scented soap onto it.

When Lyon shut off the bathroom lights and re-entered the bedroom he found Hope waiting for him resplendent in sea-green sheets. In the low light coming from under the dark shade of her bedside lamp, she looked as iridescent as the silk she lay between. As always, his heart clenched at the sight of her. He still didn't know what he'd done to deserve her, but tonight he was letting himself believe— at least a little—that this arrangement, legal though it was, wasn't temporary.

Hope's expression turned quizzical as he joined her. "That's an interesting look on your face," she said, welcoming him with her caressing touch. She lingered on the faint cropping of black hairs that reflected the other half of his ancestry. "What are you thinking about?"

"You."

"I wasn't begging for a compliment."

"It's the truth anyway. I was thinking of the kind of woman you are. How you heal your own wounds by easing those of others."

Her breath catching, Hope leaned over and kissed his chest. "Lyon...that's lovely. But sad, too. Is it because of what I asked to name the baby? If that's going to constantly remind you of losing your parents, we won't do it."

"No, I want to. I'm just floored at your generosity, making me more a part of this," he said gently stroking her abdomen.

Hope laid her head against him and stroked him with her cheek as she caressed him with her hands. "I always knew you as decent and different, Lyon, but when you say such things and show me more of who you are, I see something too tender to do the work you do."

"It's getting surprisingly easier," he said losing his fingers in her hair. "I have a little secret."

"You're going to say something sweet or too generous. Don't."

"A silken-haired seductress whose eyes forever tie me in knots."

Pushing him onto his back with a strength that shouldn't have surprised him since he knew what it took to handle animals ten and more times her weight, he was taken aback by the tears he saw in her eyes.

"Your soul touches mine," she whispered. "That probably sounds silly in this day and age, but it's the truth. Do you feel it?"

"You're precious to me."

She closed her eyes as though tasting the words. When she looked at him again, she asked, "Then why didn't you let me see who you were sooner?"

The question had been like a long-range missile, he'd known that it was coming, he just never knew exactly when. "You know why."

That grim reply silenced her because she clearly did. But he saw that she blamed herself for what didn't happen as much as for what did, and he didn't want that. "I'm no coward, Hope, but I'm not a big gambler. My assets limit me, and I'm not talking about finances. I'm talking about who and what I chose to be—as a son, a friend, and honorable cop. How could I tell you anything—a woman some elitists still believe I shouldn't touch?"

He'd noticed examples of the latter issue just recently. Every year Hope got invited to countless society functions, some of them touted pedigreed affairs. At the moment, one or two were not forthcoming. She gave no indication of being upset or even caring, but he was and did. Not for himself, but for what this could mean to her growing career in good works.

Hope, however, was shattered by what he'd shared. "If I hadn't proposed to you, you'd never have asked me out, would you?"

"It didn't seem like it would work in this lifetime." He held her gaze, but what he saw was what he'd expected his future to be—too empty and lonely to describe. Then he smiled and gave himself the gift of exploring her flawless skin. "But you're here now and as long as you are, I can't keep from reaching for you."

"Lyon…"

He silenced her by drawing her completely over him and

kissing her. His mood was as raw, his emotions as painful as an open wound. "Take me inside you," he whispered against her warm, pliant lips. "I need you."

For seconds longer he felt her resistance. She wanted to talk, to understand, to make him say things he had convinced himself that he had no right to say. But she was right—in the universe that housed their spirits, their souls had been designed to be as one. She'd recognized him before, and he was exposing himself to her now. With his searching kiss and his enticing touch he drew her away from this world of uncertainty, and into the bliss only they could create together.

Straddling him as she would one of her mounts, Hope accepted him slowly, even though she was already moist and ready for him. It just made the journey all the more poignant, a sweet torture that had him gritting his teeth and gripping the sheet to keep from leaving his imprint on her tender skin. She intensified the exquisite torment as she began caressing his chest, trailing her fingers along the collarbone he'd broken once during a game, over his hard nipples aching for her touch, down his rock-hard belly to his navel and then back up again.

When she leaned forward to wet his nipples and tease him with her mouth, he pulsed inside her, and the epithet wrenched from deep in his throat was both plea and prayer.

The movements of her hips were as graceful and smooth as though she was on a languid ride, her silken thighs holding him as firmly as she would her mount's flanks. Lyon opened his eyes wanting to watch her because that captivated him as much as her touch did. With her head and shoulders thrown back, her breasts were a superb offering and he worshipped her with his hands, then devoured her with his mouth.

Needing her liquid heat again, he drew her with him against the pillows and headboard, until her body rested completely against his. Pulsating deep inside her, he could feel her inner muscles clenching while her eyes grew low-hooded as she gave herself up to intoxicating lure of release.

"Kiss me," he said locking her against him with arms that ached to own and keep her.

"Yes," she whispered, her fingers moving over and through his hair. But her kisses were butterfly caresses that flittered over his cheekbone, along his jaw, between his eyebrows, and then the corner of his mouth. "Yes…yes…"

"For the love of heaven," Lyon groaned, *"Kiss me."*

Hope clasped his face between her hands and gave him what he wanted. With a groan of relief he drove into her. He couldn't hold her close enough, couldn't plunge himself deep enough to assuage the heavy ache. The desperation was upon him, but ecstasy was advancing. She rode them both to the edge and over and he heard her cry out his name and felt her shatter in his arms.

My heart. My life. My love.

They hovered in that place as long as possible, almost ceasing to breathe to prolong each delicious sensation. Then, although muscles relaxed and the fever ebbed, he couldn't bear to release her.

Coaxing her head onto his shoulder, he stroked her hair in apology. "Please…at least for a little while. You're comfortable, aren't you?"

"There are no words," she murmured against his neck.

As he felt her drift off to sleep, he drew up the sheet, extended his right arm and switched off her light. He lay there in the darkness a willing sentry guarding and warming what was most precious in his life.

His own lids were growing heavy when he felt a tiny kick against his abdomen. His heart swelled anew, his throat ached as emotion rose there straining for release. Slowly, with excruciating care so as not to rouse the dream in his arms, he reached down to lay a soothing hand over Hope's child. "Sweet dreams, little Meredith," he whispered.

Chapter Nine

For Christmas, Hope convinced Lyon that they should hold an open house. She explained that she always had one anyway, but at the office. Since her assistant Freddie would be taking her vacation over the holidays and would be out of the country, relocating made all the sense.

And then she got the idea that Lyon should invite everyone from the department. Lyon joked that while they were at it, they could invite the city council, too, but Hope thought it a brilliant idea. It would show how Lyon held no grudges, was well liked by his people, and that they were a happy couple.

Lyon asked, "Why can't we just send out smiling photo Christmas cards?"

Into early November, he kept trying to talk her out of it. At first he cited the strain on her pregnancy, and when that didn't do any good, he insisted that it was too much work for her regardless of how organized he had to admit she was—and, no, having Molly's able assistance didn't change his mind.

That's when Hope called upon one of her newer clients, divorcée Lara Conti. This was exactly the kind of exposure Lara's fledgling catering business needed to trigger word-of-mouth and get her more bookings. By the time their lunch meeting was over, Lara had the job and Hope knew she had gained another strong ally in town.

The open house was held the Saturday before Christmas and would begin at seven in the evening and would go until ten o' clock. By seven in the morning Hope, Lara and her mother Geraldine, and Molly were hard at it in Hope's kitchen.

Saturdays had become Lyon's indulgence time when he liked to linger in bed—preferably with Hope by his side, have coffee with her while reading the Dallas newspaper and Hope's *Wall Street Journal,* and basically play the day by ear in that give-and-take way they'd comfortably fallen into. But on Party Saturday, Hope was out of bed before the slightest hint of daylight peeked around the windows' mini-blinds. When he warily entered the kitchen at seven-thirty, the place looked like an understaffed soup kitchen.

Lyon politely greeted the ladies…and with papers under his arm, drove into town hoping the coffee wasn't already too thick at the station and that not all of the donuts were eaten.

Hope was in the bathroom putting the finishing touches on her makeup when he returned around five that evening. "Hey," she murmured as he stopped in the doorway to softly whistle at her.

"Woman, what are you on that you can look like that at seven months after being on your feet for ten hours?" he demanded.

"The vitamins Dr. Winslow put me on help, as does yoga, but—" closing the tube of mascara, she came to him and lifted her face for a kiss "—I highly recommend having a patient and understanding husband, too."

After a brief, but possessive kiss, Lyon said, "It would have been nice to hear *stud muffin* somewhere in all of that."

"I didn't want to get my imagination and hormones all hot and bothered when there's so little time," she told him in apology. "How was your day?"

"Far easier and less exciting than yours." Lyon took hold of her hands and held them out to inspect her dress. She wore a red velvet empire dress with long tight sleeves that ended in a point at her wrists. With the gold chain in her hair that dangled a teardrop ruby on her forehead, she looked like medieval royalty. Matching stud earrings completed the image. "You're breathtaking. I'm not sure I want my men within five miles of you, but like the rest of this place, you look like a fairy tale come to life."

Gently wiping lip gloss from his lower lip, Hope smiled. "I would have loved for everyone to bring their children, but with so many people, it would have been impossible to monitor them properly and to avoid accidents."

"Good point. We forgot just one thing—call for the EMTS to have a truck stationed outside. I glimpsed the food on my way through the kitchen and it's nothing short of a cardiac patient's last meal dream."

"Well, it's not a party unless the tummy gets pampered. I told you Lara is good. And wait until you see the heaping trays of shrimp and crab legs that are chilling."

When Hope met her, Lara had been an abandoned mother of three. The divorcée was living with her widowed mother Geraldine as she tried to dig her way out of debts and back taxes incurred by her two-timing ex-husband. No bank would touch her to help her launch a catering business, so Lara would bake in her mother's kitchen and go from store to office with her products, trying to garner enough interest to keep her family fed and clothed. Once she tasted Lara's quality product and saw how she paid attention to making packaging attractive, she sat the woman down in her office and said, "Show me your business plan." The rest, as the saying goes, was history.

"I'll have to arrange for a 211 call from the station to clear out my crew. It'll take at least a robbery to keep them from acting like they're at a feeding trough. You were too generous, sweetheart."

"There'll be plenty for everyone. But that reminds me— did you arrange for someone to bring your relief dispatcher a plate? Who's on duty this evening?"

"Maggie Greer. She all but begged for the job. She just lost over fifty pounds and wants to keep it that way."

Deep in thought, Hope tapped a red fingernail against her lips. "Then be sure to bring her one of the centerpieces afterward. She'll be able to use the crystal vase for years to come."

Lyon kissed her again. "As I said, too generous. So how many do you think will show? You have enough food for five or six hundred."

"Considering the list and add the spouses or dates…somewhere around 250-300."

"If they all come at once, Tan will have a nervous breakdown trying to keep parking under control."

"I know, but I've been to these kinds of events before and somehow it does seem to work out. You need to start getting ready and I need to get into the kitchen," she said

beginning to unbutton his shirt. "The girls will be returning at any minute to start the final preparations."

"I wish you would have saved yourself unnecessary
stress and not invited Clyde and Mercy," Lyon said.

Leaning forward to breathe in his male scene, Hope
then touched her lips to his chest. "I appreciate your pro-
tectiveness, but it was simply smart strategy not to snub
them, just as it was to send my father an invitation, too. I
doubt they'll come."

"You know I'll support you since at least he's a blood
relative, but if he marries Summer Isadore as rumor has it,
you can cut your ties with my blessing."

"He has a right to be happy I guess," she said. She took
his hand and drew him farther into the bathroom toward
his closet where she had a new sports jacket, dress shirt and
dress jeans hanging pressed and ready for him. "Do you
mind that I took the liberty?"

"Mind that you thought about me when you've been
working for weeks with this party and decorating on top
of your already busy schedule? Yeah, I'm ballistic."

Hope's body was humming with happiness when she
returned to the kitchen. As much as she was looking
forward to the party, she couldn't wait until tonight when
everyone went home and she could return to Lyon's arms.
They were growing closer with every day and becoming a
more intricate part of each other's lives. She couldn't ask
for anything more—except for the words a woman in love
had a right to own.

No, she told herself, she would not let herself get depressed or worry about that now.

The back door opened and a hesitant voice called, "Am
I too early?"

Molly entered and immediately took off her bright red wool coat exposing a green velvet dress with seed pearls sewn around the collar. It was Hope's Christmas present to her along with a set of pearl earrings.

"You're right on time and how lovely you look!" Hope said clapping her hands in delight. "What did Tan say when he saw you?"

"He cut me this from his greenhouse." She turned and pointed to the delicate gardenia in her hair above the bow that Hope had bought her so she could have her long hair tied back.

"Oh, how romantic. You're going to help the house smell so good."

Her blue eyes huge as she looked around, "It smells that way already. I told Tan—wait." Molly had to stop herself and think a moment. "Tan said to tell the chief that he will be outside at the front gate by 6:30."

"I will, and I'll remind Lyon that Tan needs the reflective vest he said he wanted to wear."

"He already did. He brought it to him last night—and the police radio and flashlight." Molly giggled, but looked proud, too. "You should see him. He's acting like it's the whole uniform, he's so proud."

Grateful to have such dear and helpful people in her life, Hope assured her. "Well, he's playing a vital role even if it doesn't get too crowded all at once out there. We've had a wet autumn and if people are allowed to drive anywhere they please, we'll have to start the landscaping all over come spring."

Molly looked stricken. "I didn't think of that—but I bet Tan did."

Patting her back gently, Hope redirected her focus.

"Let's start putting out the candles in strategic places, but we won't light them until we hear Tan on the radio Lyon put in the kitchen that he's taking his position. Do you know where your lighter is?"

Molly gave her a confident nod. "In my apron pocket in the kitchen."

"Wonderful. And while we're placing the candles, let's start plugging in the lights. This way when Lara and Gerri arrive, we can start setting out platters as they prepare them."

The slender woman headed for the kitchen repeating the directions to herself. Lara and Geraldine arrived about fifteen minutes later looking confident but excited and promptly put on their aprons bearing the Conti Catering logo.

By the time Lyon joined them, soft Christmas tunes were playing on the stereo, the tree was lit in the bay window in the living room, a small fire was burning in the fireplace, and Hope's lifelong collection of Christmas decorations created a fantasy world around the house.

"I hardly recognize the place," Lyon said planting a kiss just above the jewel on her forehead. "Where have you been keeping all of this stuff? The life-size, animated St. Nicholas at the front door for instance?"

"In one of the sheds behind the barn, carefully boxed and labeled," she added.

Rubbing his hands together, he said, "Shouldn't I be getting on with my job as the official food sampler?"

"If Lara or Gerri see you stick a fork in anything before the first guests arrive, they're apt to stick a fork in you. Go to the kitchen and they'll have you over your daily calorie limit before you know it."

The first to arrive were Lyon's people. Hope noticed that the men were a little reserved at first and, although the wives were wide-eyed and thrilled to be in what they considered a mansion, they were ready to find fault with her if they felt too awkward around her. Having traveled that road many a time since her school days, Hope welcomed everyone with the same warmth and enthusiasm. She'd made a point to query Lyon about each police officer's family and memorized names so that as she showed the ladies to the guest room to hang their coats and pointed out the guest bathroom, she seasoned her descriptions with, "How's your youngest, Elizabeth? I think Lyon told me that she needed tubes in her ears?" then "We thought about your Roger and some of the others being diabetic, Nancy. The dessert table has several desserts prepared for the no-sugar guests."

Kent and Shana arrived with the less-than-enthusiastic newspaper editor Tim Pettigrew in tow. That startled both Lyon and Hope, and they knew Tim had inveigled himself into an invitation when Shana rolled her eyes as she stood behind him. As they'd recovered, Gerri planted herself in front of Tim with her tray of hors d'oeuvres and with humor and southern charm declared, "Hello, Tall Drink of Water. You look parched with those pinched lips and in need of feeding."

Despite his sour-disposition, the newspaper man eyed the appealing treats with something close to lust. "If you think you can get free advertising out of this, you're sorely mistaken."

Nonplussed, Gerri batted her false eyelashes at him. "Sugar, what I was thinking is that if you ate one or two of these salmon-chive with fennel goodies right in line to the I in Conti—" she shimmied to indicate her right breast "—you'd trust me enough to show you some real treats in the kitchen we're saving for our favorite guests."

For a second, Tim looked as though he was about to charge for the front door, but suddenly he threw his head back and laughed. "Can't see how a bite or two would hurt," he said.

Teagues and Roberts exchanged bewildered looks as Gerri led Scrooge personified off to new experiences.

Within a half hour there were at least forty-five people scattered about, and at the top of the next hour three times that.

"I told you that you were spoiling everyone," Lyon said in her ear when they reconnected at one of the few vacant corners in the house. "No one wants to go home."

"It's Christmas and everyone is tired of politics and conflict." Hope eyed the crowd with pleasure. "Isn't everyone getting along nicely? It's been fun seeing chemistry in the works. See the forty-something Hispanic gentleman by the painting that I got at the auction?"

"The conspicuous guy standing alone and bored?"

"What's conspicuous about him?"

"He's the only person here that's in a full suit."

"Rafael Simone. My client, thank you. I've been meaning to introduce you, but we keep getting pulled in opposite directions. He manages the fish counter at the supermarket."

"There is no fish counter at the supermarket. There's some packaged stuff due to FDA laws about keeping beef, chicken, and seafood separate and most of it looks like it traveled to Texas via a rowboat from Australia."

"But he dreams of there being one, or a little shop in town. He dresses impeccably because five days a week he deals with fish in a place that really doesn't care about fish. We're working on his dream." Hope tightened her fingers on his sleeve. "I'm waiting for one of my widow ladies. They were talking earlier."

As Hope scanned the crowd, Lyon studied her. "Has it crossed your mind that he brushed her off and he's waiting for you?"

Frustrated, Hope directed his attention to the opposite side of the room where two people stood seemingly in rapt conversation over the igloo art beside the punchbowl. "Fine. Here's one you can't deny. Have you noticed your detective—"

"Sweetheart, you're allowed to look and sound like royalty from another era. I'm a chief not a chieftain. He's not *my* anything."

Hope stroked his shoulder. "I'm making a point. He's sought her out several times this evening. You said he's not much for mingling and prefers field work."

"His divorce was tough on him. He's probably intrigued with the physics of how she kept the ice clear so you could see the inside with the battery-operated fire display and the other figurines." Belatedly he allowed, "She's a pretty woman."

"He seems a very serious type. Look at how he listens to her. That's a plus."

"Hope."

"All I'm saying is that a nice-looking man, who seems to hang on her every word, is a nice change of pace for her. She doesn't need another 'Don't worry about it, honey' con in her life again. Nor do her kids."

"Table that." Taking hold of her shoulders, Lyon turned her toward the front entrance. "This requires your focus now."

Hope's gaze settled on what was getting him all tense. Her father and Summer had just entered the house. "I don't know how I can," she told him. "That image defies the logic of everything inside me."

Lyon slipped his arm around her waist. "Take a deep breath and know I'll be right beside you."

As usual, her father was his own fashion statement, wearing a black velvet tuxedo jacket and ruffled shirt over jeans and boots. Summer wore a black leather bomber jacket and pants with a red sequin tube top. Her ever-changing hair—today eggplant—was piled on her head with practiced indifference.

"Merry Christmas," Hope said as they reached them. "How nice of you to come. Father." Once he took the unlit cigar out of his mouth, she gave him a polite peck on the cheek.

"Hope, honey," Summer gushed. "Aren't you look-ing…ripe. When did you say you were due?"

Taking Hope's hand in his and giving it a gentle squeeze, Lyon said, "Her doctor is actually concerned that's she's on the lowest end for acceptable weight gain."

"You've never looked better," her father scoffed. "What's wrong with that doctor?"

"She's an excellent doctor and very dedicated to her patients' care," Hope replied resting her head against Lyon's shoulder. It had been dear of him to try and shut up Summer. "She did recommend I cut *one* activity from my routine for these last several weeks." She gave him a sidelong look because he knew exactly what that might include.

"I vote for shutting your office," he said keeping his ex-pression blank. "The yoga and the rest are all good for you."

Clearing her throat, Hope redirected. "You're looking well, Dad."

"When my doctor told me to lose ten pounds, I cut back to two cigars a day."

The only person who seemed to think that was funny

was Summer. Perturbed, Ellis narrowed his eyes at Lyon. "Well, you're still here."

"Plan to keep it that way, too," Lyon replied with a feral smile.

"At least you don't scare easily, I'll give you that." Looking bored with the conversation, Ellis scanned the room. "Quite the turnout."

Looking unhappy with the way the conversation had been going so far, Summer sniffed. "But is there anyone here *we* can talk to?"

With something akin to a growl, Ellis pretended to flick ashes on top of her hair. "Well, hell, Summer, honey, you pretend to talk to me all the time. What's the difference?" He ignored her double-take and demanded "Where's the bar?"

"No bar." Lyon nodded across the room. "We have a facsimile of beer and a punch for the ladies with a touch of champagne. We want to make sure all of you make it home safely tonight."

Ellis looked like he smelled something bad and then patted his left pocket. "No matter. I always travel prepared." As he drew a lighter out of his right pocket, Hope grabbed it.

"Hey!" her father snapped.

"I don't believe you," Hope muttered. She directed both index fingers to her tummy. "Hello? Pregnant! I'll return it as you leave."

"Go find me a glass with some ice cubes," he told Summer. "Cubes, not that chipped crap. Don't crack the skin on that," he added to Hope pointing at the cigar she held out of his reach.

As he walked off, Lyon took a restless hold of Hope's shoulders. "Better hide that thing from me," he said. "I'm about to snap it into half a dozen pieces and toss it into the flowerbeds."

"Sure," she replied, "pollute my shrubs."

By 9:30 p.m., Lyon considered lighting the cigar himself—right under one of the smoke detectors. He was happy for Hope that things had gone as well as they did, but he was ready to clear everyone out. Attendance was down a bit from what she'd expected, but some of her older clients hadn't shown up. Considering the hours they'd scheduled, they'd known that was a possibility. The Nichols had stayed away, too, but that was fine. One thing Hope could take pride in was how people lingered, especially his crew. And maybe she was right about Cooper and Lara. The detective was spending as much time in the kitchen as in here with the other guests.

Laughter caught his attention and he saw Hope and Molly assisting one of the elderly clients up from a couch. Mrs. Dillinger, he thought, with an amused smile. Who was going to have trouble remembering a chauffeur-driven millionairess with a name like that? He went to offer his aid.

"It was delightful, Hope, dear," the woman said as she steadied herself with the help of several hands and her cane. "Next year a little less conservative with the champagne. I don't have to worry about driving."

Hope laughed then put a cautionary finger to her lips. "Not so loud, Mrs. D. My husband the cop is within hearing distance."

The wiry woman gazed up at him with bright eyes that declared she was free of cataracts. "Hello again, good looking. You don't have a twin brother, do you?"

Raucous laughter followed them out of the house. At the

sight of them easing down the sidewalk, her driver bolted from behind the wheel, opened the back passenger door and jogged up the sidewalk to take over.

"I have her, sir," he told Lyon.

"This is Wilmington," Mrs. Dillinger said releasing Lyon to pat the arm of the elderly chauffeur. "I've buried three husbands, buried two children, and made, lost, and made fortunes—the latter with help from your darling wife—but I've only had one chauffeur, eh Bobby?"

"Yes, ma'am. Good night, sir," he said to Lyon.

Wilmington wasn't much taller or younger than she was, but he was agile and caring, and clearly devoted to her. As they drove away, Lyon wondered if there was something more between them, then he shook his head. Hope's romantic nature was starting to rub off on him.

Although it was getting seriously cold now that the latest Blue Norther had pushed through, Lyon shoved his hands into the pockets of his sports jacket and walked down to the gate. Tan had slipped on the heavier coat he'd brought with him and wore a skier's wide headband, too.

"Come on inside," he said, shaking the shorter man's hand.

"I good, Chief," Tan replied, but he was bobbing in place like a boxer warming up for a fight. "I wait for all car to leave."

There were only five left and the catering van. "That's Hope's father's car, and the others belong to my officers. Even after they leave, it'll be another hour or more before the van leaves. Your work is finished. Come inside and let Molly get you a hot toddy or something."

"Thank you, Chief." As they walked together, Tan said, "Molly say party very good."

"She's right. Hope should be pleased. How did that radio work for you?"

Tan patted the handheld device with his gloved hand. "A-OK! Detective Jones teach Molly how to use. I think I get radio for us. Easier than driving across pasture. Good to check on Molly."

"You're right. It's a very smart idea. I'll tell Hope. We'll get them for you."

They had reached the sidewalk and Tan was thanking him effusively when they heard a scream from inside the house, then another and then yelling. Lyon's hand went immediately for his weapon, but, of course, he wasn't wearing a gun tonight, and with a house full of cops, he told himself it shouldn't have been needed. But what if Hope had fallen or been hurt somehow? He and Tan ran the rest of the way.

When they burst inside, everyone was still, but the tension in the room told Lyon what the screams had. Something had gone wrong.

His gaze encompassing, Lyon took in Summer Isadore cowering against one wall and looking like a train wreck with her hair falling, her mascara bleeding down her face and her nose bleeding. Buddy Yantis stood watching her as though ready to intercede if she threw herself toward Ellis. Ellis Harrell was being held against the opposite wall by Officers Juarez and Scott Laurie.

Cooper Jones standing between them had apparently started trying to gauge what had happened. Everyone else, including Hope, stood back, their expressions reflecting utter shock. As soon as Molly saw Tan behind him, she hurried to him. Lyon briefly glanced at Tan and motioned for them to get to the side and out of the way for precaution's sake.

Sobbing and clutching her hand to her chest, Summer shouted, "I'm going to sue you, you pig! You broke my nose and my w-wrist."

"It should have been your neck," Ellis snarled back at her.

"What happened?" Lyon demanded advancing toward them. He saw Hope begin to speak but gave her a look that stopped her.

Cooper situated himself on the other side of Summer to give Lyon clear scope, but gestured toward the master suite. "There was a scream from back there. As Juarez and I started to investigate, Mr. Harrell came barreling out of there dragging Ms.—" He glanced at Summer and then at Hope with uncertainty.

"Isadore," Hope supplied. "She was already bleeding from the nose," she told Lyon.

"She fell into the vanity," Ellis added.

"You hit me!" Summer declared.

"Come here and I'll show you the difference," he growled.

"Ellis!" Lyon's rebuke won his father-in-law's silence, although the older man continued to look like a predator unhappy with having only achieved half of his goal. "Did you hit her?" Lyon asked.

"Yes!" Summer declared. "I want to press charges."

"She fell."

"You pushed me!"

Ellis gave Lyon a satisfied smile. "Ah. Finally the truth from the alley cat's own mouth."

Pinching the bridge of his nose, Lyon asked wearily, "Why?"

"If your bulldogs would allow me, I'll show you."

"No stupid moves," Lyon said pointing into his face.

"You have my word." With that the two officers took a step back and Ellis slowly extended his clenched right hand, then opened it.

Hope gasped.

"Yes," Ellis said. "This diamond bracelet was my wife's and now belongs to my daughter. I gave it to Rebecca for our tenth wedding anniversary. When I heard that tramp complaining to Hope that she couldn't wait for the other bathroom to be free, Hope graciously offered her own." He gestured toward the master suite. "After what seemed like more than adequate time, I became suspicious and went to investigate. That's when I found her rifling through my daughter's things."

His speech was growing more slurred indicating to Lyon that as adrenaline faded, the effects of the alcohol he'd consumed became more apparent.

Turning to Summer, Lyon asked, "Is that true? Did you take it?"

"It was just lying there on the counter. I was only admiring it. The truth is, I thought it was fake."

"Liar!" Ellis roared. "You—"

"Easy now," Buddy Yantis warned. "You're in the presence of ladies."

"I think," Hope began slowly, "that if you will see to Summer's medical expenses, Father, that we can agree it was just a bad misunderstanding."

"No way!" Summer shouted.

Hope picked up several paper napkins from the nearest table and brought them to her. She said quietly, "The bracelet wasn't on the counter."

"Oh, fine. My word against the Chief of Police's wife. Talk about a stacked deck."

"If you want to keep up that attitude," Hope replied, "I think you should understand that I'm within my rights to have you taken down to the station and strip-searched by the department's female office, Maggie Greer."

"Miss Hope is right about the bracelet," Molly said clutching Tan as he held her to his side. "I clean for her. I mean Mrs. Teague. She keeps her jewelry just the way her mama did hers. She told me when she was teaching me how to do my job and where everything goes. Everything is boxed with the papers included. Nothing is ever left out. This way nothing can fall down a drain or get lost in the carpet."

Hope returned to Molly and touched her shoulder. "Thank you, Molly."

Seeing that she was trapped by her own lies, Summer started wailing. "That's not fair! Why should you get everything and I get crap? You don't even like him!" she declared pointing at Ellis.

"You're right," Hope replied. "Sometimes I don't like him at all. But he's my father, which is the only reason you were invited into this house. That courtesy won't happen again."

Lyon nodded to Juarez. "Can you and your wife take this woman to the hospital and either have her treated or admitted, depending on what the x-rays show? I don't trust her being alone with one officer in the car."

Juarez's wife stepped beside her husband. "We'll do it, Chief."

"I'll be his backup," Scott Laurie said.

Lyon thanked them all and while Vince's wife, Alicia, got their coats and Hope got Summer's things, he took the two officers aside and gave them additional instructions, then apologized for costing them additional hours away from home. But Scott reminded him that he was single, and Vince said his mother-in-law was babysitting and that Alicia would call once they got to the hospital and explained things to her.

"My things are at the ranch," Summer whined, annoyed at being virtually ignored. "I demand my things."

"I'll see you get them tomorrow," Hope said.

The party had officially ended. As soon as Summer was taken from the house, Hope went to her father and put her hand out for the bracelet. Ellis was slow to hand it over.

"I remember the night I gave it to her," he said. "I thought my heart would stop from looking at someone so beautiful." His gaze settled on Hope. "I know I've been a disappointment to you. It shouldn't make any difference to you, but I've come to realize that I'm a disappointment to myself."

Slowly, Hope reached into her father's pocket and took out the sterling flask. Shaking it, she found it empty. "Lyon," she said, "can you see he gets home, too? I'll call Greenleaf and warn him of their arrival."

"I'll do it," Cooper said.

Lyon said, "I'll follow in his car and you can drop me off back here."

Despite it only being a few miles away, it was a good half hour before Lyon and Cooper returned. Seeing the Conti van in the last stages of being loaded, Cooper said he would help them and then make sure the ladies got home.

Lyon went inside and found Hope putting out the last candles and pulling the plug on the Christmas tree. When she saw him, she came into his arms.

"Where's Molly and Tan?"

"I sent them home right after you left. I think she was as upset as I was." She sighed heavily. "Things had been going so well."

Lyon tightened his arms. "The party was a smashing success. Don't let what Summer did take away from that.

Maggie radioed me from the station and said the buzz was so cool she could kick herself for missing it. She asked if we'd do it next year."

"That's nice. But right now I don't think I'll ever want another party again."

"You're exhausted. Let's go to bed. The rest can wait until tomorrow and I'll help you."

But as they entered their bedroom, Hope held back. "I hate the idea of that woman being in our room."

"Let's change the sheets. That'll make you feel fresher." Lyon doubted Summer had done anything there, but knew she would be more comfortable.

While they worked, Lyon told her how wonderful the party had been, reported all of the compliments he'd heard, how much the wives liked her, how she was right about Cooper and Lara. She made polite responses and only displayed real emotion when she spoke of how Tan had cradled Molly against him when she had the courage to confirm where the bracelet was kept.

"What if Summer sues?" she asked abruptly.

"She won't," he replied. "In fact I'll bet she leaves Cedar Grove pretty quickly. Who's going to have anything to do with her if Ellis Harrell won't have her?"

"At least there's that. And here I was convinced she was about to be my stepmother."

"Your father apologized to you again."

"Okay." Suddenly she shivered. "I'm cold. I think I need to sleep in a warm gown tonight."

She went to get changed. Lyon followed and hung his things, then watched as she began spraying the counter and scrubbing at it with a washcloth. That was followed by her closing the sink drain and washing the bracelet with soap.

When she started at the closet doorknob with a sanitary wipe, he'd seen way too much.

"Hope." Taking the towelette away from her, he threw it into the trash and put the disinfectant spray under the sink cabinet. "That's enough. Everything is clean. She's gone."

Turning off the lights, he lifted her into his arms. "Come to bed, little queen." He carried her there and laid her between the fresh-scented sheets, quickly following. Shutting off his light, Lyon eased up behind her aligning their bodies and wrapping his arm around her to caress the firm mound where the child rested.

"Has Meredith been quiet tonight?" he asked, partly out of curiosity, partly to keep her from thinking of tonight's ugliness.

"Yes. Except when Summer screamed and my father roared. Then we both jumped." She covered his hand with hers.

Lyon thought she would drift off to sleep then, but he was wrong. Her breathing stayed the same and he knew she was staring at the closed mini-blinds, yet seeing the sad end to her wonderful party.

"You're not going to get any rest that way."

"I know." Sitting up, she tugged and wrestled with the gown. "This is suffocating me," she said. "And I can't feel you."

Lyon helped her and smiled as she flung the soft white flannel to the chaise at the foot of the bed. Then he let her show him how close she wanted him. When she lifted her leg over his and gently urged him to come inside her, he pressed an open-mouthed kiss to her neck.

"Are you sure?"

"Always."

He made slow, sweet love to her warming her from the outside until inside she burned with a fire of her own. He gave her all that he was because in giving, he received everything he needed in the world.

Chapter Ten

Christmas and New Year's passed quietly. Two days before the first holiday, Hope came down with a cold and stayed wrapped in a blanket on the couch sleeping most of the time. For New Year's, Lyon took his share of the shift work since there was a big party over at the grill, and several other bashes at some of the big estates in the area. He'd made sure Kent put announcements on the radio and in the newspaper that the department would be out in full force and that seemed to help keep arrests down this year. They ended up with only two DUI cases and one assault.

Hope spent New Year's taking down all of the Christmas decorations and wrapping and boxing everything. Tan and Molly offered to help but she insisted they spent New Year's Eve together. She did let them come over on New Year's Day and while Lyon caught up on lost sleep, they transferred the mountain of boxes to the storage shed for another year.

The next week she and Lyon began the natural childbirth classes held over at the junior college. There were seven other couples and Lyon got teased a bit for being the "senior" member of the group, but he took it good naturedly. He still wasn't too sure about being in the delivery room with her, though.

Summer didn't sue, although she continued to claim that she had a case to anyone who would listen. There were fewer and fewer of those, as the truth about what was behind her breakup with Ellis Harrell got around. Business at her store dropped, as well, which Lyon saw as indicative to how beloved Hope was in the community regardless of how anyone felt about Ellis or him. In the end, Summer sold her remaining inventory to another shop in town for pennies on the dollar, and Hope purchased the building that had been a divorce settlement from her third marriage. The last Hope heard, Summer moved to Memphis.

Hope was preparing to lease the building to Lara Conti for a fraction of the going rates in the area. They agreed to a one-year contract at which time they would review the books and see about what were the best options all around. Frankly, Hope was planning on selling her the building. Lara already was booked solid for Valentine's Day, had one Easter Egg Hunt Party, and one engagement party slated. She'd never looked happier, and Hope knew part of the reason was that Cooper was spending a good deal of his free time over there and Lara's boys thought the "CSI" man was super.

Gerri was having less success with Tim Pettigrew, but he didn't exactly run in the opposite direction when they happened to cross paths. "I'm giving him another month to play hard to get," she told Hope during their last chat, "and then I'm going to fish in friendlier waters. You'd be surprised how that can change a man's way of thinking."

Hope had heard that theory but was glad she didn't have to test it. She wasn't all that happy that Pettigrew might be who Gerri wanted; however, she was willing to play wait and see as Lara was resigned to.

There was no question that Lyon was right where he wanted to be. Three little words remained unspoken between them, and yet she was more content in her life than she'd ever been. She'd begun to conclude that maybe words were sometimes overrated. Almost.

During the second week in January, the steady pattern of cold weather intensified and Cedar Grove, along with all of North and East Texas suddenly found itself under a winter storm warning. It had begun to snow on the way to the office and by midday that had turned to freezing rain, then ice, then freezing rain again. Hope sent Freddie home only an hour after she'd arrived and was planning to lock up herself as soon as she finished the report she'd been working on. However, it was difficult to concentrate when her mind kept wandering to Lyon. He'd had to testify at the county court this morning and she wouldn't relax until he returned home.

When her phone rang, she grabbed it hoping it was him—and she wasn't disappointed.

"Hello, beautiful. Why am I getting you at your office? You should be home," he said.

"I'm not there because you're not here," she said looking out her office window. "Where are you?"

"Just now entering the city limits. Man, it's been rough. Some parts of the county have lost power and it's only a matter of time before we do. The ice is getting so heavy on trees and lines, when branches pop it sounds like gunfire, and the dead trees are wiping out pole after pole. If I passed one electric cooperative truck, I've passed a half dozen. You aren't wearing any of those sexy high heels, are you? One fall and you'd shake Meredith loose for sure. We'd never get you to Dr. Winslow's hospital on time."

She adored him for thinking of the baby as much as he did her. "I'm wearing my most comfortable Uggs with the nonskid bottoms," she assured him. "Not to worry. Are you coming by here or do you have to head to the station first?"

"We're going to get you home. I'll probably have to be out and about with the rest of the guys until this ends, so I want to see that you have a good fire going and that the generator is gassed up in case you do lose power over there."

"If you're pressed for time, Tan can help me do that," Hope replied.

"He would be proud to, I know, and I'm grateful for that. But he has Molly, and we need to rely on him to keep the horses fixed up with fresh hay, and—damn."

"What's wrong? Lyon?"

The phone suddenly switched to dial tone. Hope disconnected, too, and waited for the call back...and waited. When the phone rang again, she exhaled with relief.

"You scared me. What happened?" she asked.

"Hope? It's Buddy here at the station. Listen, the chief wanted you to know something's come up and he's going to be delayed. But he doesn't want you to worry."

If ever sillier words were ever spoken, Hope thought, her insides going from churning to clench. "Well, I can already hear trouble in your voice, Buddy, so you might as well tell me what's going on."

"Somebody's stuck on the ice and the chief needs to help him get out."

By now, Hope was out of her chair and moving from window to window to see what she could. When she got to the side window facing the south part of town, her heart shot up and lodged in her throat. "Oh, my God!"

"Blasted, Hope. You weren't supposed to go look."

Almost at the last traffic light a pickup truck was spinning and sliding sideways to try and champion the subtle slope in the road, but the thin ice was deceiving and there was no traction for the tires. To make matters worse, the power line could actually be seen starting to slowly tilt into the street. If the driver of the truck didn't move soon, he would be stuck under the downed pole and live lines—and the driver was her father!

Right behind him was Lyon in his patrol car striving to help him gain momentum and push through.

Hope hung up on Buddy and shut off her computer. Grabbing her coat and shawl, she locked up the office and hurried down the street as fast as she could given the weather and her own condition.

Despite the town being reduced to near ghost-town status, several people had already collected to watch the unfolding drama. When they saw her, she noticed winces and some grim exchanged glances.

"You shouldn't be out here in the cold," Matt Plummer told her. His barbershop was just to their right. "Come inside, honey. I'll get you a cup of hot tea."

"Thank you, Mr. Plummer, but I need to—" To do what? Wait and see? Watch the pole crush her father in his cab or electrocute him? "—I'll be fine," she said hugging herself as she began to shake from fear, not cold.

"There's no time, Chief! That pole's coming down," someone said.

"Look!" someone else said. "The chief's doing good. He's pushing him through."

Hope realized that was the plan just as the words were spoken. "Oh, no," she whispered pressing her gloved hands to her lips. They couldn't both make it. Didn't Lyon see?

Of course he did, she thought with her next breath. But that was his job—to help people, even if those people didn't like or even despised him.

In almost slow motion she watched with despair as Lyon eased back down the road and then shifted into drive. His chained tires would be useless on mere black ice, but on this composite mess the traction let him accelerate and using his reinforced bumper, he nudged the pickup into forward motion. But with every foot forward, the pole inched down.

Suddenly, the truck shot forward, but as Lyon tried to do the same, the pole landed with a sickening thud on the squad car's roof. The small crowd reacted with groans and one-line observations to relieve their own tension.

"Is the line touching the car?"

"Look at that! It's inches from the roof."

"Maybe if he could crawl over the seat and try to get out the back door…"

"I saw a spark from the transformer. He better not."

Hope had to shut out the voices. She would say something ugly or burst into tears if she didn't. She could see Lyon through his windshield and knew he could see her. She kept that eye contact as her lifeline.

Her father had parked a safe distance away and climbed out to see what had happened only to clasp his head with his hands.

Grateful that he understood the sacrifice on his behalf, Hope called, "Dad! Over here."

He slid and stumbled over to her. To his credit, he looked like he was about to have a stroke and Hope's heart softened toward him.

"I told him not to do it."

"It's his job," Hope replied her gaze back on Lyon.

Sirens sounded and Vince Juarez arrived to order people back to make room for the fire truck coming. He saw Hope and came toward her.

"Don't ask me to move, Vince," she said polite, but determined. "I'm not budging."

"I know, Mrs. Teague, but if I didn't at least try, the chief would have things to say if—"

Hope sent him a laser look.

"When he's freed. Sorry, ma'am."

"Are the electric people on the way?"

"Yeah. ETA maybe five minutes. They'll get him out."

Hope's hold on her emotions were slipping. "In time," she said forcefully. "I'd like him not to look like burned bacon."

Vince had to turn away. "Hurry up," she heard him mutter under his breath.

When Lyon indicated his cell phone to her, she showed him that she had hers and in a moment, it rang.

"Hey," he said his voice gruff. "What are you doing out here?"

"What are you doing *there?*"

"Guess my timing was a little off. Look, sweetheart, I'd feel better if you weren't watching this."

"Me, too. But do you think I can walk away?" Her voice cracked and she was ashamed because he didn't need the added pressure.

"Oh, baby...I know."

There was just silence for a minute and Hope watched him rub at his face and then check the wires again.

"Sweetheart, I need you to know something."

No! Not like this. But she forced herself to smile through tears and said, "Yeah, Chief, you do."

"Things have been getting pretty transparent—"

"A lot transparent."

"I know I've been holding out on you," he said with the same voice he used to tell her how he was going to make love to her before he did it. "But only for the best intentions."

"Don't you realize I don't want anyone but you?"

"So my skull is thicker than some. I just had to be sure, you know?"

"I know."

"And now I can't even say it with you in my arms."

"Please wait. Please tell me when you can do that."

As more ice fell, a larger spark erupted from the transformer at the top of the pole. There were several gasps and a scream. Hope knew it wasn't her because she had her hand clamped to her mouth and was gritting her teeth.

She heard Lyon breathing trying to control himself, as well.

"Hope," he said his voice almost guttural. "I love you. I love you with all I am and all I hoped to be."

Tears of joy and anguish washed down her frozen cheeks. "Come back to me," she whispered.

Then she felt a cramp that had her bending in half. "Oh! Lyon—oh, no..."

"What is it? Hope, is it the baby? Give the phone to Juarez. Hope!"

* * *

When Hope opened her eyes again, she was looking at a white ceiling that had a water stain in the corner. Something needed to be done about that, she thought drowsily wondering why she'd never noticed it before. Then a middle-aged man with glasses and wearing a white jacket blocked her view.

"There you are," he said, smiling. "How do you feel?"

Unless angels wore pens in their pockets, she told herself that she wasn't dead. "A little queasy. A little sore."

"You fainted."

It all came rushing back and Hope had the worst impulse to heave. "My husband! Lyon. I have to get back. Can you tell me—?"

The doctor vanished and an instant later, Lyon was hovering over her and lifting her into his arms. With a cry of joy, Hope hugged him fiercely.

"You're alive!"

He didn't reply right away. He was more intent on kissing her until they were both trembling. After that the first thing he said was, "I love you."

"I love you."

That required another long embrace until her machines and his racing heart settled down. During that time, Lyon made sure that he accounted for most of the hairs on her head, half of the bones in her body, and the peacefulness in her womb.

"The baby is fine," he said at last. "You just had a bit of system overload from the stress. You'll have to rest for a day or two to be sure, but we can get you home as soon as I sign your release."

"Home. Yes, please."

In barely an hour, Hope lay in Lyon's arms before a crackling fire. The world was right side up again and had never been more beautiful to her. She'd felt so blessed, she hadn't taken her eyes off of him the entire drive home.

Apparently the utility people had arrived just as she was fainting and had him out of the car before Vince and her father could carry her to Vince's patrol car. Lyon wouldn't wait for an ambulance and had held her in his arms the whole way.

Her father had stayed in the waiting room for news. When they emerged, he simply pressed his hand to his chest. But when he started to leave, Hope stopped him.

"Come here."

He stopped before her a tortured man. "I didn't mean to intrude. I just wanted to thank the chief again."

"His name is Lyon. He's your son-in-law."

"You must hate me."

It had been tempting at times. But Hope had new life in her—and love. She wouldn't let hate taint that.

"You can't talk the way you do, like you have done in front of me since as long as I can remember," she said. "I want Meredith to be a child, not an adult before her time like I was hearing things no child should hear. I want her to have a grandfather she can be proud of, not afraid or ashamed of."

Ellis had bowed his head both troubled and ashamed. "You're naming the baby Meredith?"

"Meredith Rebecca, after her grandmothers."

Her father nodded his head and his eyes filled. "Those are good names."

Touching his hand, Hope said, "We'll talk in a few days."

"I would like that," he said gravely.

Now, warm again and dry, having changed into a pink cashmere sweater and black jeans, she snuggled in Lyon's arms and kept stroking his chest to reassure herself that he was real and that this wasn't a dream her mind locked her in to hide from grief. He was here, strong and *alive*.

"Why did you make me wait so long to hear those words?" she said on a moan. "You knew how I felt about you."

He brought her hand up to his lips for a kiss. "I knew you liked me. I knew the sex was fantastic between us. I thought you might be falling a little in love with me, but…I worried that it was a rebound thing. Then, as I told you, I felt you deserved better."

"There is no one better, Lyon," she said before kissing him with all of her heart.

When he finally had to tear his mouth from hers and bury his face in the hollow of her throat, he apologized. "The doctor gave me strict orders," he told her. "We can't risk intercourse until you see Dr. Winslow next week."

"You're talking about sex," she told him. "We'll only be making love. Lyon, wasn't it that all the time?"

"To me it was," he said crushing her against his chest. "And I wish I had the words to tell you how that was a dream come true for me because it was always you, all along." He leaned back to stroke her face with his fingertips. "I was devastated when Will decided he wanted you. I even tried to hate you for not seeing what he was, but I couldn't."

"I'm glad."

"I knew that evening in the bar that I couldn't let you marry him. I don't know what I would have done, but you need that truth. Then when the truck exploded and you collapsed in my arms, I was too badly burned to do more than catch you for a second. The soul mates you spoke of—I saw mine in your eyes then. I wanted to carry you away from there and never let you think of him and your time together again." Lyon shook his head. "I'm not that different than your father, my love. There is and only will be one woman for me."

"I've been so blind. So foolish for not seeing how you felt."

"Why didn't you take a risk and ask—or tell me?" he teased.

Hope arched her eyebrows. "Lyon Teague, I am born and raised a southern woman. My mother came from Spanish nobility. We don't say it first."

Lyon's chest shook with laughter. "That didn't stop you from proposing."

She glanced at him from under her lashes. "Well, I didn't say we didn't know how to go about getting what we wanted."

His gaze fierce with love and dreams, Lyon leaned over to kiss the place where he last felt Meredith kick, and then lifted Hope against his heart. "Never let us go," he said.

"I promise, my love," Hope replied.

* * * * *

Kay Young returned to woozy consciousness to find that she was lying on a soft sofa beneath a heap of quilts near a cheerfully burning fire. When she tried to move, however, everything hurt, and she groaned.

At once she heard a sound, then a stranger with a hard, harsh face was squatting beside her. "Shh," he said softly. "You're safe here. I promise."

"I have to go," she said weakly, struggling against pain. "He'll find me. He can't find me."

"Easy, lady," he said quietly. "You're hurt. No one's going to find you here."

"He will," she said desperately, terror clutching at her insides. "He always finds me!"

"Easy," he said again. "There's a blizzard outside. No one's getting here tonight, not even the doctor. I know, because I tried."

"Doctor? I don't need a doctor! I've got to get away."

"There's nowhere to go tonight," he said levelly. "And if I thought you could stand, I'd take you to a window and show you."

But even as she tried once more to pull away the quilts, she remembered something else: this man had been gentle when he'd found her beside the road, even when she had kicked and clawed. He hadn't hurt her.

Terror receded just a bit. She looked at him and detected signs of true concern there.

The terror eased another notch and she let her head sag on the pillow. "He always finds me," she whispered.

"Not here. Not tonight. That much I can guarantee."

Will Kay's mysterious rescuer protect
her from her worst fears?
Find out in HER HERO IN HIDING
by New York Times *bestselling author Rachel Lee.*
Available June 2010,
only from Silhouette® Romantic Suspense.

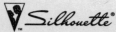

ROMANTIC
SUSPENSE

Sparked by Danger, Fueled by Passion.

NEW YORK TIMES AND *USA TODAY*
BESTSELLING AUTHOR

RACHEL LEE

BRINGS YOU AN ALL-NEW
CONARD COUNTY: THE NEXT GENERATION SAGA!

After finding the injured Kay Young on a deserted country road Clint Ardmore learns that she is not only being hunted by a serial killer, but is also three months pregnant. He is determined to protect them—even if it means forgoing the solitude that he has come to appreciate. But will Clint grow fond of having an attractive woman occupy his otherwise empty ranch?

Find out in

Her Hero in Hiding

Available June 2010 wherever books are sold.

Visit Silhouette Books at www.eHarlequin.com

SRS27681

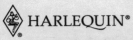

HARLEQUIN® Romance®

GIRLS' Weekend in VEGAS

Four friends, four dream weddings!

On a girly weekend in Las Vegas, best friends Alex, Molly,
Serena and Jayne are supposed to just have fun and forget
men, but they end up meeting their perfect matches!
Will the love they find in Vegas stay in Vegas?

Find out in this sassy, fun and wildly romantic miniseries
all about love and friendship!

Saving Cinderella! by MYRNA MACKENZIE
Available June

Vegas Pregnancy Surprise by SHIRLEY JUMP
Available July

Inconveniently Wed! by JACKIE BRAUN
Available August

Wedding Date with the Best Man
by MELISSA MCCLONE
Available September

www.eHarlequin.com

HR17663

REQUEST YOUR FREE BOOKS!
2 FREE NOVELS PLUS 2 FREE GIFTS!

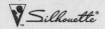

SPECIAL EDITION
Life, Love and Family!

YES! Please send me 2 FREE Silhouette® Special Edition® novels and my 2 FREE gifts (gifts are worth about $10). After receiving them, if I don't wish to receive any more books, I can return the shipping statement marked "cancel." If I don't cancel, I will receive 6 brand-new novels every month and be billed just $4.24 per book in the U.S. or $4.99 per book in Canada. That's a saving of 15% off the cover price! It's quite a bargain! Shipping and handling is just 50¢ per book.* I understand that accepting the 2 free books and gifts places me under no obligation to buy anything. I can always return a shipment and cancel at any time. Even if I never buy another book from Silhouette, the two free books and gifts are mine to keep forever.

235/335 SDN E5RG

Name _____ (PLEASE PRINT) _____

Address _____ Apt. # _____

City _____ State/Prov. _____ Zip/Postal Code _____

Signature (if under 18, a parent or guardian must sign)

Mail to the **Silhouette Reader Service:**
IN U.S.A.: P.O. Box 1867, Buffalo, NY 14240-1867
IN CANADA: P.O. Box 609, Fort Erie, Ontario L2A 5X3

Not valid for current subscribers to Silhouette Special Edition books.

Want to try two free books from another line?
Call 1-800-873-8635 or visit www.morefreebooks.com.

* Terms and prices subject to change without notice. Prices do not include applicable taxes. N.Y. residents add applicable sales tax. Canadian residents will be charged applicable provincial taxes and GST. Offer not valid in Quebec. This offer is limited to one order per household. All orders subject to approval. Credit or debit balances in a customer's account(s) may be offset by any other outstanding balance owed by or to the customer. Please allow 4 to 6 weeks for delivery. Offer available while quantities last.

Your Privacy: Silhouette is committed to protecting your privacy. Our Privacy Policy is available online at www.eHarlequin.com or upon request from the Reader Service. From time to time we make our lists of customers available to reputable third parties who may have a product or service of interest to you. If you would prefer we not share your name and address, please check here. ☐

Help us get it right—We strive for accurate, respectful and relevant communications. To clarify or modify your communication preferences, visit us at www.ReaderService.com/consumerschoice.

SSE10R